Additional P

With this hypnotic collection, Nadir Ali conjures the lost art of truly immersive story-telling and reminds me why I fell in love with reading in the first place. These are settings, characters, and situations rarely seen in contemporary literature and woefully absent from the bookshelves of the English-speaking world, but they cry out to be known. Ali brings them unforgettably to life with empathy, wisdom, and subtle sensuality. These stories will haunt you in the best way.

- Chaitali Sen, author of *The Pathless Sky*

Hero, is a collection of quick and fast paced short stories that read like character studies. The first person style of writing lets readers into the lives of dynamic and colorful characters. The poetic language lends depth to the narrative.

-Stewart Shaw, author of *House of Men: poems*

What a beautiful collection of stories by Nadir Ali, in his book Hero and Other Stories. Such a pleasure to read the lyrical prose and come to learn about the rich lives of the characters as they build relationships with one another and navigate the world and customs around them.

-Devi Laskar, author of *Circa* and *The Atlas of Reds and Blues*

For Nadir Ali writing fiction was an act of rediscovering one's own existence, finding broken bits of history and then making sense of it. Spread over a vast stretch of time, his stories bring to life the lives of the ordinary, the lovers, dacoits, thieves, hookers, ironsmiths, wrestlers, missing from official records.

-Zubair Ahmad, author of *Grieving for Pigeons*

ISBN: 978-0-9843776-6-4

Weavers Press © 2022

Cover design by Amna Ali
Artwork by Amna Ali

Weavers Press is dedicated to publishing quality
works of literature. Weavers Press prefers to publish
writings by and about South Asians but will consider
other works if they center important issues or
marginal voices.

Hero and Other Stories

'In loving memory of Nadir Ali and Razia Nadir'

Hero

and

Other Stories

NADIR ALI

Translated by
Amna Ali and Moazzam Sheikh

Weavers Press
San Francisco
www.weaverspress.com

چندن رُکھ لگا وچ ویڑے، زور دھگانے کھہِۓ وو

شاہ حسین

*A sandal tree grows in the courtyard, why
the violence?*

Shah Husain

Table of Contents

Introduction   i

Baba Sheenah   1

Twins   8

Grapes   16

Feeqa's Death   20

Hero   26

Nooran Niari   32

The Saint of the Sparrows   37

Bala Flatulent   44

Balwant Kaur   51

The Newspaper   58

Qissa Shah Husain   61

Mangta the Sarangi Player   71

Hussaina Qaachu   76

Bundu, Consoler of the Rich   82

Introduction

Nadir Ali and his Fiction

I came to know Nadir Ali's writing through sheer stroke of luck. I had been asked to edit/ translate a book of short stories by Pakistani writers for Penguin, India. Without fully grasping the scope of the project, I laid down a condition: the book would represent most languages of Pakistan, not just Urdu and English. My contact at Penguin agreed. I reached out to a friend, who put me in touch with his youngest sister, Amna Ali, my future wife, whose father, Nadir Ali, was a well-respected Punjabi fiction writer. My own knowledge of Punjabi literature was almost nonexistent by then despite it being my mother tongue simply because Pakistan's ruling elite has decided to not teach Punjabi in school at any level. By the time the Penguin book came out, Amna and I were already married. For me, knowing Nadir Ali is synonymous with embracing modern Punjabi fiction. I was also fortunate enough to have spent a lot of time with him, as he and his wife visited us in San Francisco regularly until his health wouldn't allow it, and of course I visited Lahore as well. We had innumerable conversations about all things under the sun, women, sex, booze, notions of beauty and morality, friendship, culture, religion – but above all history and literature.

He was one of the most well-read persons I have ever met, and his reading shelves contained western to Indian history, philosophy, and literature, with tremendous in-depth knowledge and understanding of classical Punjabi literature, including the poetry by the Sikh gurus. His deep study of Punjabi was largely thanks to the weekly gatherings at poet, playwright and critic Najm Hosain Syed's house. His association with Najm and the extended Punjabi *sangat* lasted over forty years and was held in deep reverence by him.

In the right setting, he could opine on the importance of Dostoevsky's speech in honor of Pushkin and in the same breath wax eloquent on Nabokov's gushing over Romain Rolland's *Jean-Christophe*. A humanist at heart, his preferred lens was that of Marxism, although he had no problem criticizing the soul crushing Soviet-style communism just as he wouldn't shy away from pointing out the dehumanizing side of American capitalism. He was a man of culture and admired the flexibility of traditions, with very little respect for religious dogma. His sense of humor delighted those around him. He once told his wife, who insisted that he tag along on a pilgrimage to Mecca, that instead of wasting money and time in Saudi Arabia she could cast her stones at him. Although he didn't care much for western music (my one big criticism), Indian music - classical, semi-classical and early era film songs – was etched into his soul since he insisted that poetry was nothing but singing. And that's where we differed. We also differed on how short stories should be created. He was fundamentally a poet and it is important to take note of that fact in order to understand his fiction output, which outgrew his poetry, even if we don't include his non-fiction, which was serialized in his favorite Punjabi literary magazine *Pancham*.

It's widely agreed that all creative work is a result of the creator's unconscious mind - what and when the unconscious mind unlocks, no one fully understands - but poetry and revelation are like twins. His stories, short in length barring a few exceptions, came to him as a revelation as if he was receiving a poem via two fundamental sources: Dreams and actual people. One could call them prose poems, but that would be missing the point. He was not the kind of a writer, for example, that I am, though I did learn from him a lot. His stories, by and large, did not come to him because, generally speaking, an idea suddenly seized him, though ideas are part of his stories. The point I am trying to convey here, based on countless discussions with him on the art and craft of short story writing, is that he didn't believe in creating or crafting a story. It often came to him in a dream; and other times, it came to him through a real person, who would embody an idea and become a central character in the story. Just as not every dream turned into a story, a person whose appearance triggered the story must've also struck an uncanny note. And the dreams which yielded to stories were always fundamentally about people, but as opposed to the stories directly inspired by the people on the street or family, the dreams evoked memories. For example:

I had a peculiar dream last night. I am the kind of man who always thinks deeply about dreams. When I lost and then initiated the arduous task of recovering my memory, I went in search of all those times I could not account for by raking through my dreams.

Despite being in love with life, Nadir Ali came to writing as a broken, haunted man. A man whose mind could not stop wondering why things went wrong. Partly because he lived in a society where at the time certain questions could not be raised loudly and partly because of his complete break- down after the 1971 war, he found an outlet in his stories, but before that could happen, he had to rediscover his deep love for the Punjabi language. His emotional trauma, it seems, could not be expressed in his poems and he found that the short story format was more suited to what his heart wanted unleashed. His stories attempt to fathom man's moral breakdown while they also hope to make sense of the complexities of life from the point of view of a child and adolescent, then as a young and old man. First, there's the bloody partition, then Bangladesh's War of Independence, and finally the breakdown of traditions, values, society's moral compass, loss of touch with nature. It is safe to say that though he left his village, his village never left him. The village of his childhood was a place where a human being learned to strike a respectful balance with other humans, animals and nature. And that desire to achieve inner harmony kept a leash on a person's greed, selfishness and narcissism, one of the recurrent motifs in his stories. Circumstances beyond his control disrupted his inner harmony and things began to fall apart. In my opinion, his stories *Saint of the Sparrows* and *Qissa Shah Husain* are his attempts to go back in time to the roots of his literary culture and analyze the forces which disturb and disrupt a place's political and emotional life, and also what tools a society employs to maintain its sanity and dignity.

If life had been kind to him, he would've become a professor of history or literature, but in order to get married to the girl he'd been in love with since the age of 11 and then support his family he considered that joining the army as a cadet was his best option, though it was a common option for many young men of his time. If he hadn't joined the army, his wife once lamented to me, he wouldn't have witnessed the butchery of Bengalis by West Pakistan's army. And if he hadn't witnessed the killing, he wouldn't have lost his memory. If he hadn't lost his memory - and gone through medical treatment, electric shocks, mental asylum - he wouldn't have felt the rage and intense urge to go searching for things lost in space and time. And I believe it was because of this feeling of intense personal loss, that he began to sense a loss much bigger taking place right before everyone's eyes. In the realm of culture, traditions, humanity, nature, friendship, all in the name of development, progress, and modernization with an inhuman capitalist push. He began to notice people utterly cut off from their own history partly due to education promoted by the colonial syllabus and later the collusion of Pakistan's own ruling elite, rigidly maintaining an outdated infrastructure of a three-tiered education system. None of Nadir Ali's grandchildren, with whom he was extremely close, can read or write in Punjabi. His own children would speak Urdu with him and among themselves.

Although his stories have a very wide canvas, his recurrent concerns are few. There are no heroes in his stories, nor villains. He's drawn to people, who despite disadvantages and hard times, maintain dignity or win another person's respect as the characters in *Feeqa's Death* and *Bundu, Consoler of the Rich* show. The women in the stories *Twins*, *Nooran Niari* and *Balwant Kaur* are not tragic figures to him but those who show resilience. The partition of India left a scar on Nadir Ali's consciousness and though it may not appear directly on the page, its repercussions can be felt in many stories. In love with the common man and woman, he abhorred dividing people along religious lines as it did more harm than good. The elephant in the room, however, was the army action in what was then East Pakistan. Call it guilt or trauma, it affected him so much that you won't find a single direct mention of it in any of his stories if memory serves me right, but after a careful reading, you'll find the traces of tragedy and cruelty in almost all his stories.

In *Bundu, Consoler of the Rich,* the narrator, a professor at a college, recalls a time when Bundu the washerman took extra care to make sure the narrator's clothes were spick and span even when he could not pay Bundu for his services, a selfless act which eventually results in the narrator's getting transferred first to Lahore and later to East Pakistan.

Bundu played an important role in my transfer to Lahore when our principal accepted a position at the university and took me along. "You are the best-dressed man in all of Gujrat!", the principal had said. From Lahore, I went on to Dhaka University in 1965. My children and I took to Dhaka, but luck was not on our side. We were spared the perils of detention in 1971 as we were able to come to West Pakistan for the summer holidays. But I remained affected by 1971. I became very ill. I lost my memory during treatment. Once recovered, I made a trip to Gujrat after a gap of twenty-five years. Bundu had passed away by then.

The story starts with a dream the narrator has in which a Bengali woman appears to take a walk with him to a grave. Then, one day, he realizes that the Bengali woman had Bundu's eyes. Of course, we know that he went to East Pakistan not as a professor but Major Nadir Ali and was made under complex circumstances the commanding officer of a battalion, until he was sent back to Pakistan months before the Pakistani army surrendered. Concerns in

Bundu's story also bounce off the title story *Hero* whose protagonist attracts the attention of the narrator, again a professor but this time Professor Nadir Ali. The hero of the story is a man who despite his poverty has a style about him which foremost shows up in his nicely trimmed and ironed clothes, and of course how he returns the professor's greetings. The fact that the hero lives inside an abandoned temple scores a political and emotional point about guilt and trauma. Bundu and the protagonist of *Hero* are but two sides of the same coin.

Also, in *Feeqa's Death*, when the protagonist says, recalling an older incident and making sense of his dreams, "Feeqa had committed a murder which only Hussaina Mehr and I had witnessed . . ," Nadir Ali the writer allows his readers a rare window into his pain of having to watch Bengalis being murdered by the army.

Nadir Ali's stories were not easy to translate despite the deceptive simplicity. He invented his own syntax and idiom and didn't care about formalities and literary conventions. And like in *Autumn of the Patriarch* by Garcia Marquez, one of his favorite writers, the readers have to be very careful and do a writerly reading to discern the many voices as they pretend to come out of one mouth. Amna Ali went above and beyond in making sure there were no errors left especially with regards to logical progression of the narrator's casual but circular storytelling technique. As all translators are wont to do under difficult situations, we took some liberties so the translated text reads smoothly in the target language. In some cases, we had not much choice but to do away with quotation marks, both double and single, as it became clear, time and again, that all the voices bounced off the walls of a single madhouse. Both Amna and I are deeply indebted to the help given again and again by the real heroes of modern Punjabi fiction such as Maqsood Saqib, Nain Sukh, Zubair Ahmed, Ijaz, and Mudassar Bashir among others. We hope these complex and compassionate stories will delight and enrich the reader. All shortcomings the reader will encounter must be attributed to the translators.

Baba Sheenah

What drew my ancestors to the godforsaken mountains of the Salt Range[1] remains a mystery. They might have been fugitives, hiding from people they once plundered, or perhaps escaping plunder themselves. Stories of thieves and dacoits are popular even today. They were portrayed as folk heroes in the early part of the twentieth century, when I was a child. Thieving and stealing back then was different from the daylight robberies common now and criminals did not have patrons among the rulers. Thieves and dacoits were also somewhat benign in those benign times! They were mostly the powerless and poor, perhaps desperate for some semblance of power. As far as I could tell, a poor person's life meant wielding a stick against endless attacks. Let go of the stick and you are history.

Perhaps poverty was born in Chakwal and grew taller as it climbed up the hills to where we lived. We could have gone on to loot lands further and further out, had the British not enticed our cash starved people to become soldiers. We stole everything in the army too, including weapons, though stealing old army blankets and mosquito nets did not have the noble status that hustling cattle enjoyed. My own

---

[1] A system of mountains and low hills in northern Punjab rich in salt deposits

family reflected the changing times. My father became a soldier and Uncle Sheenah remained a dacoit. This happened around the time of the first world war, when most recruits from our parts were soldiers. Subsequently, many rose through the ranks as officers. Previously destitute Rajas and Maliks lorded over the area by the time of the second world war. I grew up listening to stories of Uncle Sheenah. Moreover, I took it to heart when my mother mentioned that I resembled him and I began to copy him.

Old Man Sheenah, my mother's elder brother, had been an erstwhile hero from our area. Naturally, he was my hero too. His story was largely forgotten though. His wife drove him out of the house, and as a retiree he lived alone, some miles from his village and about ten miles from ours. A few square yards of stony fields belonged to him and he extracted a rough, hard living from them. He was never invited anywhere and rituals of mourning and celebrations of marriages passed him by. He was a born loner. Nevertheless, he was my hero. I took after my mother's side of the family and was no stranger to poverty and struggle. I could boast of being not only a good student, but also a skilled horse rider by the time I turned fourteen. Sheenah was a famed horse rider, so riding became my first love. Once I grew confident and was allowed to ride out alone, I decided to pay Uncle Sheenah a long overdue visit. A good ten years had passed since I had last seen him.

Sheenah's abode was hardly more than a shack. He

got by with the help of a donkey that would fetch water from a rivulet down in the valley, and an emaciated but well-bred horse. Sheenah had aged noticeably in the last ten years. My people were not effusive in greeting each other, but even among the quiet, my uncle was quieter and appeared aloof though he was ever alert. He sat twisting some strands of rope and without taking a break he addressed me. "Hello, Achchoo, is all well back home?"

"All is well, dear uncle!" I replied. "Since I had the horse for a day, I took the opportunity to visit you. I've been wanting to look you up for years!"

"Restrain your mare and let her graze. Get yourself some water. There is some bread lying around too. I didn't cook anything. There isn't much to eat and I sold the cow when it stopped giving milk," he said, with an air of familiarity.

He patted my head as I moved in close and touched his knees. He enquired after my school and a few of the old folks from the village. We sat quietly together for a long time. If someone chanced upon us, he would see two people not talking so much as dropping an occasional word now and then, much like an old roof leaking during the rainy season. 'Drip!' followed by a long pause, then 'Drip!', like the rhythm of life in the salt range. My uncle seemed to enjoy the music of silence.

"The sun will set soon. Night riding isn't easy. You better leave if you're not staying the night," Sheenah suggested as evening advanced.

Thus ended the most unforgettable day of my life.

3

I felt taller and older as I rode home. I entered the house energized. As usual, my mother sensed the change and pounced on me. "Where have you been Achchoo? You seem excited."

I revealed that I had seen Uncle.

"How was he? Don't go looking for trouble now. Keep your mind on your studies. Idle people end up without a penny to their names!" my mother warned.

"He was fine!" was all I said in reply.

Two more months passed and my uncle stayed on my mind. Every time I galloped across the plateau, I pretended to be Sheenah. "Come on, you old horse of Sheenah!" I would shout as the horse raced. On my next visit, I brought him some grains and a lump of jaggery. He was not fond of the hookah. He seemed more relaxed this time and asked, "How is everyone in the village?"

"Uncle, the entire village has enlisted in the army!" I replied.

"Good for them, at least they will escape the clutches of their women! Tell your dad to enlist too!" he joked.

"Uncle, you ran away from Aunty too!"

"Child, I escaped from humans when I was very young! A thief leads a lonely life." He said, opening up to me for the first time.

Such meetings with Uncle Sheenah went on for two years. Mother would also enquire about him now and then. I didn't need my uncle's permission to visit. He seemed to look forward to my arrival. I had lots of time on my hands after completing my matriculation exams. One day I made the excuse of

4

visiting Chakwal and decided to spend the night at Sheenah's instead. There was no electricity there. In the evening, it quickly turned dark and quiet like the dead of night.

Uncle appeared more relaxed at night. I was eager to learn more about his life. "Uncle, have you ever killed a man?"

"What do you know about killing, little fellow? The answer is yes and no!" he revealed in a riddle.

"Achchoo, you are old enough now, and a smart kid. Perhaps you will understand. It began when a young man from the village Mughnee eloped with the daughter of a powerful chieftain of the Rajas from village Kullewaal. The chief's old man was my friend and reached out to me. He wanted to regain their clan's honor by killing the young man from Mughnee who was also a Raja, but much poorer. 'We have already tried and failed two times,' he said. 'I will give you anything you desire if you carry out the killing.' Hired assassins were unheard of back then. Old friends came to each other's rescue to settle vendettas or restore honor. But killing isn't a one man operation normally. I hired two musallees[2] to help me and did not let them out of sight thereafter."

My uncle went on to explain that no one was privy to events of that night besides those two. He was sharing his story because I was old enough to understand. I felt a foot taller just knowing that he chose to reveal his secret to me!

"I surveyed Mughni one day to get a lay of the

---

[2] Low caste villagers usually entrusted with less desirable tasks like cleaning, etc.

land," he continued. "The young Raja had built an eagle's nest for himself, atop a steep cliff and far from the rest of the village. There was a sheer fall on three sides of the house. The fourth side had an easier entry but it was probably well guarded. I chose a moonless night in the following week for the attack and trained the two men to climb up the steep cliff and to the rooftop. I planned to go inside myself and their job was to create a ruckus on the rooftop so the Raja would get distracted, making him an easy target for my deadly strike. If I needed any help, they would come to my rescue. Achchoo, I was an expert at stealing into a room, as if I was invisible!

I disappeared among the cattle coming home in the evening, stole into the house and hid under a bed. I knew the thief's craft. You have to be quick and patient. You lie low like a snake hibernating, then strike! Quick and deadly!

The young man came into the room late in the evening. He lit the oil lamp. Then he produced a small round mirror from his pocket and stared into it as he combed his hair. I was the snake, but somehow he became the snake charmer! My mind wandered while on a mission for the first time ever. 'What a beautiful person! And how much he desires to live!' I reflected. My resolve took an about turn and my grip loosened on the javelin. I came out of hiding and faced him. The young man had the expression of one who could see his end. I saw death reflected in his eyes. But he was a brave one and spoke up. 'Get it over with Malik! And don't harm the women if you call yourself a man. You can finish her off as she won't survive the shock in any case!'

"Nobody is going to raise a finger to hurt you, Raja, now or ever! Tell the women not to raise any alarm and let me leave peacefully," I replied. My companions had jumped into the yard and held their axes on the ready. "Hold it!" I ordered, pointing my javelin at them. "Nobody is going to touch him ever!" The musallees followed me out of the compound.

The Raja and his woman are still alive. The other Rajas bitterly protested with me. They even tried to have me killed. No one harmed the young man. I was changed forever! I gave up the life of thievery. It held no attraction for me. I am a solitary man but a happy one, Lord be praised!"

Old man Sheenah cut a saintly figure despite never fasting or saying his prayers. He fell ill around the time when I was commissioned into the army. I brought him to my place and he lived for ten more years. But he never told this tale to anyone else and never revisited it with me.

Translated by Amna Ali

Twins

Many people struggle to make sense of the twin brother phenomenon and we twins ourselves were no less puzzled by it. If Basheera felt pain, I felt it too, yet I also lessened my own pain by annoying, even hurting him occasionally. When a certain behavior of ours puzzled people, they would say, and I would concur, that it must be because we were twins. That headache only got worse once we started school, though my father never bought into the belief about twins. He maintained that it had to be the shared experience that created our bond. After all, he explained, he had five brothers, not born on the same day, yet they had a similar uncanny connection and could feel what the other was going through. Despite lacking formal education, he believed in analyzing things rather than accepting tales people spun. That analytic mind of his was thrown into confusion when Basheera went off the rails around seventh grade. While Basheera's condition did not improve, I developed a reputation - just as my father had predicted - for being a good student. I also won scholarships in eighth and tenth grades.

By the time I went to college, Basheera had grown into a handsome young man though something was still off in his head. He could go on without an incident for a long stretch of time. Father managed to involve him in hunting expeditions and he turned out to be an excellent marksman. However, if a bout of madness snuck up on him, he would refuse to step out of the house for six months at a time. Providing food and medicines for him was never an issue as we owned more than a thousand acres of land, half of which belonged to him.

When Basheera reached marriageable age, my uncles advised my father to reach out to the elder Chaudhry Ahmaa, who was his childhood friend and belonged to our village, to ask for his only daughter's hand in marriage to Basheera.That would also help ensure that Ahmaa's lands were taken care of. Chaudhry Ahmaa had initially asked me to marry his daughter, but I excused myself saying I would not marry for another eight to ten years, not until I had finished my studies and passed the civil service exams.

Chaudhry's daughter, Shado, had known us since childhood and agreed to marry Basheera even though she knew about his illness. "Even if you decide to push me into the well, I will honor the love between our fathers!" she said. Our extended families even had a running joke about how difficult it would be to tell Basheera and Muneera apart!

I was hesitant at first, but then I thought perhaps marriage would do Basheera some good. After all, didn't society consider marriage a kind of medicine? As the wedding date approached, Basheera's mental state steadily improved, convincing me that I had been correct and I threw myself into the preparations. Bad luck caught up though, and he decided to completely lose it just when the wedding day arrived. The more vexatious he became, the more we were convinced that only marriage could save him now. Desperate to salvage the situation somehow, we sedated him with medicine before the wedding procession left for the bride's village. Four strong men were tasked with propping him up as well as keeping him under control lest he became agitated.

By the time the bridal palanquin arrived at the groom's place, his fits had subsided. The wedding turned out to be a big deal. Almost the entire village had shown up. It was our family tradition to sacrifice a goat before the bride set foot onto the compound. That time we had three goats brought to our place for the auspicious occasion. Being a family of hunters, we were used to killing chickens, but I had also been slaughtering the sacrificial goats on Eid for the last several years. The butchers would comment on the dexterity with which I slit the goat's throat with one swift swipe of the knife, while onlookers recited praise of Allah! I located the artery effortlessly and immediately cut it. Such peace I would find in the act of slaughter!

The moment the palanquin arrived, I lost no time in slaughtering the three goats. The butchers took care of the writhing goats. But today I had given no thought to my white shalwar kameez, which had turned red, the color of the bride's wedding shawl!

Shado wept as she entered the house. My mother gently admonished her, "Don't weep since it is not a good omen!"

I grew irritated and retorted. "There is much

crying in store for her. Her arrival alone is a good omen. We are the unworthy ones!"

We rushed through the rituals meant to be performed upon the bride's arrival. Basheera still appeared a bit unhinged. I remained anxious. Who would pour oil to anoint the already dead! I quieted down the singers and servants by handing a wad of cash to them. Already past midnight, the journey from Samundri had been a long one.

Two separate quarters had been built, one for Basheera and one for me, beyond the central courtyard of the house, and even though mother arranged for a communal tandoor, we stuck to our own living areas. Gas-powered lights brightened Basheera's portion of the house that day and still desolation hovered all around. I felt for the first time, deep in my heart, the injustice meted out to the bride! Right above the entrance to Basheera's portion Al Basharat[3] was inscribed in big letters, but that day it seemed someone had mocked us by writing that. All of a sudden, I heard a loud banging on the door followed by Shado's cries. When I rushed to intervene, my mother blocked me, saying it was not the night to meddle in their affairs.

"Four strong men had to keep him under control all day; how is a single Shado supposed to manage by herself?" I reasoned. "No one else has to do anything. I will go inside and lock Basheera in a separate room if need be."

Shado stood sobbing inside and said that Basheera

---

[3] Glad tidings

had tried to push her out into the courtyard before storming off to the back room where he locked himself in. She was trembling. I walked over to the back room and locked it from the outside. I cannot explain what transpired next, but I locked the front door, too, from the inside. I switched off the light and told Shado to get some sleep since she had a whole lifetime to shed tears.

"You terrified me more than Basheera when you slaughtered the goats at the entrance," the words tumbled out of her mouth.

"It is you who has been slaughtered, Shado!" I said, stroking her head with pity. "Go, get some sleep now."

She refused to budge. She seemed to be offering herself for slaughter as the fourth goat. Words might have been exchanged, but it was our bodies that moved of their own volition, turning me into the groom in Basheera's place. That moment from hell was soon over. When I stepped outside, I felt as though the blood splattered on my clothes belonged to Basheera rather than the goats.

That night became a source of endless suffering for me. Sitting so far away, a heavenly breeze would blow and for a brief moment I would picture Shado, red bangles adorning her wrists. The rest of my time would be spent in a cauldron of guilt. Minor things would annoy me. I could go on talking for hours, or simply disappear for long periods and hide away in my locked room. I was in no state to sit for any examinations. Two chances for civil service exams came and went but I had lost all desire for this desolate world.

Lines from a ghazal by Bahadur Shah played endlessly in my mind, *neither the light of someone's eyes, nor comfort for the heart/ nothing but a pinch of dust, of no use to anyone.* To my surprise, the song of Shado's life played out differently. On my brief visits home, I found her in control of her universe, not the picture of a vanquished soul one might expect. Basheera meanwhile was improving ever so slightly and Shado had adopted a motherly style with him. Everyone sang praises of her courage. Even I was pampered by her, fed and looked after. Just her presence would rejuvenate me.

But before long, regret clawed its way back into my thoughts. I felt trapped; the only way out would be to snatch my heart out and hang it somewhere as a punishment. I tried to snuff out my desires, but they returned forcefully each time I replayed the moment I had crossed the forbidden line. I was not yet mad, but I was getting there. I wanted to see a doctor like Basheera's. But which doctor could I open my heart to!

I turned to hunting with more zeal. I used to be known for the quick work I made of slaughter. Now I became obsessed with the ritual. It brought me the solace I craved so desperately. It also sharpened something within me that began to cut me from the inside. I became the hunter and the hunted!

Often, I joined the farmers tilling the land when I visited the village. That helped take my mind off my agonizing thoughts. I had to wrestle with myself to finally fall asleep despite the fatigue. Back then, farmers still relied on the wooden plow. I would yoke the oxen to the plow and try to work the land. However, it was the act of hitting the oxen with a staff that gave me satisfaction.

One day my father saw my behavior and stopped me. "Haven't you heard that famous verse of Waris Shah describing Ranjha, the cowherd and lover, how he called out gently to the cow, not once striking its horns?" I felt his words hinted at the sin I had hidden away, rather than my treatment of the oxen!

One day my father mentioned that he planned to visit the water springs at Gharat near Jhelum so he could drink the water and cure his ailment. He wanted me to accompany him as he had something to tell me. I couldn't sleep for two nights, fearing he knew what troubled me.

It turned out that I was wrong. As was his habit, father retraced the story of his life as well as mine and my brother's. When Basheera was just a young boy, father had chanced upon him fooling around with another boy. It would have remained just child's play for Basheera had he not caught him and made him face a scale on which sins and virtues were supposedly weighed. The experience turned Basheera into someone who relished hitting the oxen, just as I had been doing, father pointed out. My brother also found pleasure in taking a stick and beating the poor fish swimming in the stream. "Angry and irritated at first, like you are now, he slipped into madness a year later.

"Muneera, a person's own actions can end up driving him mad. Not humans but God keeps stock of one's deeds. A person doesn't hit the ox's horns because he is mad. Rather he descends into madness because he has hit the ox's horns!" Father's words stung me for a few days. Once again I felt he was referring to the night of the slaughter. Little by little, I began to understand the subtext of his words.

No one but my father could understand the path I decided to take then. I sold my share of the land at whatever price I easily managed and built a tiny house for myself in Lahore. I spent a part of the money on further studies and some on Basheera's treatment. His condition improved. One thing I never managed to do was get married. At forty plus years of age, I was not ready to yet again slaughter the goats whose slaying set off this tragic chain of events.

Translated by Amna Ali

Grapes

The fever had been rising since morning and by afternoon my body was literally burning. Amma had been busy with me. She left for the fields with food on the late side, after dragging my cot to the shade of the chinaberry in the lower courtyard. The raging fever left me too weak to get up.

The chinaberry provided little shade, but I could not haul myself up to go inside. I had recurrent cramps and a sinking feeling in my heart. When will I get out of here? Because of fever, I felt everything in the house was about to attack me.

There was only one pillow left in the house claimed by whoever fell sick. The odor of the entire family's sweat had penetrated the pillow which consisted of two uneven lumps of cotton wool. I tossed my head on it one way, then another, but found no comfort. I turned away from the hand pump to stare at the empty kitchen, and for a moment the pillow's lower side offered peace. Only the likes of Bhag Mal had real kitchens. Our entire house had nothing in it, what to speak of the kitchen. In the evening my mother would borrow a glowing lump of coal from the neighbors to fire up the stove, but what was there to cook? Every single day the same old chickpeas. Even turnips seemed enticing now.

Amma had tried her best to persuade me to eat a little in the morning. A piece of roti with some milk.

16

She wasn't going to be thrifty or else she could've given me lassi, but one look at the milk and I wanted to throw up. I insisted on salty lassi, drank some and threw up anyway. I felt very thirsty, but I couldn't even hold down water. An empty stomach was bad enough, I felt my heart sink as well. With the fever rising gradually, my head came close to exploding. I tried the thicker end of the pillow, but that seemed to hurt my back so I shifted to the lower end.

This lower courtyard is almost in the middle of our home. The upper courtyard is the slightly higher one where our main room sits. The lower one has the handpump and underneath the chinaberry is a place for washing. There is another open space as well, next to the door to the alley, we call it the outer courtyard. It has a room that is missing one of its doors where we keep the animals. Chacha says he will add another door this winter. The house is in need of so many things. The door to the outside is also about to give way, and we need it to shut in the animals at night. Their room is always dark and dank, smelling of waterlogged soil. Our house is on higher ground otherwise it too would settle into the waterlogged soil like much of the village.

"Hai Amma!", I cried out hoping to get anyone's attention. If one cannot even cry out when sick then what else should one do? I called out again, "Hai, hai . . ." Not that anyone could hear me. The whole village falls into a coma in the afternoon. All one hears is the cry of the doves and the monotonous sound of our village's flour mill. That's all. No other sound. "Hai Amma . . ." I wailed this time.

Desperate, I went to the pitcher, and soon as I returned I vomited and felt drained of all energy. Yet the fever opened up my nostrils.

Mother had prepared some mud for plastering the walls and I detected the pleasant smell of clay brought from the loamy soil at the western edge of our village. She had also added cow dung and some hay to the mix and I felt like I could smell the dung and hay separately. I even smelt the soap lying in the washing area. Or I thought I smelt it. I wonder if all those smells floated only in my head. My sense of smell is very good in any case. I solve mysteries not by recognizing footprints but with my nose. I could tell who brought home roasted chickpeas. I could smell if someone slathered their roti with ghee two houses away. Hunger is a mighty smell too.

Today my mind hopped from the courtyard to the alley, from the alley to the city, from the city to the main bazaar. The smell of the city's sewage attacked my senses. The smell of the bricks and coals from the kilns, the foul smell of the city's garbage heaps - I could detect the smells rising from all kinds of rubbish; then back to the bazaar and the sewage. But today, after wandering around, my mind finally arrived at the fruit shop and took in the fragrances of fruits: mangoes, pomegranates, bananas, loquats, fresh smells and stale smells. I could tell each one apart, but oh amma! The grapes! I felt I could recover if only I could find grapes. My fever would break. My nausea would go away.

"Amma!" Finally, she was back.

"What's the matter?" She's never returned from

the fields in a good mood, but maybe out of regard for my illness she'd be nicer today.

"Amma, grapes!" as if I posed a riddle.

"Grapes nor poison; are Nurpur's smells paying you a visit today?" Amma teased me. "It is grape season, cruel Amma," I laughed for the first time since morning. "How well you know the season for it! Didn't I buy some for you last year?" She too couldn't help laughing. "Look, you are sweating! When your fever breaks, go to Nurpur and get yourself some grapes. I hear they are selling four annas a pao these days. Whatever made you think of grapes today?"

"I just had a craving!" I said, half in jest.

"Here, I will boil some milk for you" and with that Amma brought me closer to the pot reserved for boiling milk, back into the village.

Translated by Omar Ali

Feeqa's Death

I dreamed of Feeqa today after so many years ... The message a dream brings is unique and complex. Feeqa's case, however, is different. I had erased both his life and death from my memory. But he borrowed a new mask this time.

A water-carrier all his life, he sat today as Hussaina Mehr's helper at the fruit shop. I picked up a melon and held it out to him in the dream. But Feeqa said, 'Little master, you didn't pick up the melon from this shop, so I can't take any money for this. Enjoy!' Laughing, he turned to Hussaina Mehr, 'You haven't kept melons here, Mehr, it must belong to another shop,' and then he said to me, 'You are mistaken, boss,' and laughed. Hussaina peered inside the shop and found no melons there. The dream ended. I woke up happy with a free melon.

Dreams are strange enactments of life's song and dance. Even if we pick apart each strand of the rope, we won't understand them. This is the mistake psychologists make. They'd say it is the mother symbol or the sex symbol. But both these thrusts are wrong ... Each strand is a different song and when you knit these strands into the rope of life, each twist then manifests a different dance! The thing was that Feeqa had stolen a melon for me once from Hussaina's field which was situated behind the shops. From that point on we were always on the prowl to steal melons at night. So Feeqa had reminded me, today, of a favor from the forgotten past by giving me the stolen melon . . . But there was another twist to it too . . . Feeqa had committed a murder which only Hussaina Mehr and I had witnessed.

Swai Ram's shop was next to Mehr's. At dawn, the thoroughfare was completely empty. It was time for the cart delivering ice blocks to show up. Hussaina Mehr unloaded fruit boxes inside to stack them up. He had had a quarrel with Sheeda the ice vendor the morning before which Feeqa and I had seen. I had taken our cows to the city park, where grazing was prohibited, and was headed back at the first hint of morning. At that time, Sheeda was unloading the ice blocks and piling them up on the platform of Swai Ram's shop. Sheeda was on dope, had an ugly mug, and enjoyed cussing with his pig-like face. Mehr was a simple man and didn't like messing with anyone. 'Oh, Mehr, let me shove this little mango up your ass!' This was enough to invite trouble. Mehr grabbed a piece of brick from the shop and hurled it at Sheeda. It hit him on the forehead. Feeqa and I rushed, pushing the two away from each other . . . 'Let me go and unload the ice, and if I don't return to shove a bamboo up your ass, Mehr, I ain't my father's son.' 'Son, you don't seem to be one anyway,' Mehr dared him.

At dawn, Mehr and Sheeda were grabbing each other. Feeqa stood in the midst, disentangling them even before I arrived. Sheeda's eyes blood-shot, his temper ran high. He was a habitual criminal and

Mehr always tried to restrain him. Those were the partition days; besides, Sheeda had his eyes on Swai Ram. He even said to Feeqa a few times, 'Shouldn't we take off the bloody Hindu's dhoti?' On a few occasions, he didn't pay for the soda bottles and had also demanded twice as much for the ice delivery the last time. Scared, Swai Ram dished out the money, but complained to Mehr. The friendship between Mehr and Swai Ram was deep and time-tested.

We used to listen to the news and songs on Swai Ram's radio. Swai Ram would read the news aloud from *Parbhat* every day. Most people in the square were illiterates like Feeqa and Mehr. Swai Ram was an educated and political person. The faces of Mahatma Gandhi and the Muslim Frontier Gandhi had been painted on each side of the 'Royal Soda Water Factory' signboard 'by Sarwar Painter.' Most of us, including the painter, did not even know who the other Gandhi was.

While painting, Sarwar Painter gradually became a Muslim League leader, and while listening to the songs and reading the newspaper, I too became a neighborhood leader. See, how I have digressed . . . The digressing thread, however, has a connection not only with the murder Feeqa committed but his death as well.

I learned from Feeqa that Sheeda had cursed and challenged the moment he arrived. The whole thing spun out of control and he started harassing Mehr. The two were exchanging blows; Feeqa too got embroiled in it though his intent actually was to pry them away from.

22

I arrived at the scene shortly and immediately attempted to disengage them. Suddenly, Sheeda's hand reached for the cart. The ice-pick was in his grip, 'Sheeda's holding the ice-pick, Feeqa!' I cried in alarm.

Mehr was an older man and heavy-set, but Feeqa was simply lightning made flesh. He twisted Sheeda's wrist and, grabbing the pick, stabbed him three times in the chest. The blood left its splashes on Feeqa's and Mehr's clothes. Blood poured out of Sheeda's nose as well and he fell back, writhing. He raised his hand in the air once, then went cold.

'What the hell has happened, Mehr? He's dead.'

Though I was the youngest, I hadn't become the neighborhood leader for nothing. 'Run, you two. No one has seen it.'

Feeqa was shit scared. It had all happened in a flash solely because of his speed. Come to think of it, he had not quarreled with Sheeda. But he was a loyal friend, and his friendship was deep with Mehr. He used to sprinkle water in front of everyone's shops including Mehr's. He filled their pitchers as well, but of late there was not much demand for a water-carrier. Mehr always helped out and looked after him.

Well, what had to come to pass had already happened. Mehr and Feeqa both ran off. I felt unusually brave standing at a distance. There was no one around. The first few horse-drawn carriages were about to arrive . . . The early morning walkers were usually Hindus; however, they rarely came out of their houses for walks in the terrifying summer of

1947.

I tethered the cows. As I looked out from the rooftop, I spotted a tongawala shouting aloud, 'Murder, there has been a murder!' Mehr sauntered out of his house slowly and mingled with the crowd. Feeqa too had filled his water sack again and, after a fleeting glance, began sprinkling the street as though nothing had happened. I was impatient to reach the place of action and, telling Mother about the commotion at the corner, rushed over to the spot to take a second look at Sheeda. His eyes were wide open and the open flaps of his dhoti had left him denuded in the front. Dhurrey Shah, the tongawala, who was the big bad boy of the neighborhood, covered the front and said, 'Someone's finished him off. Mehr, go and break the news to his family. We'll catch the murderer, rest assured. What mother-fucker would've dared to do this in our neighbor-hood? Sheeda's murderer must be from another village. I know them well. Dhurrey Shah is still alive.' He went on with his sermon.

Feeqa, Mehr, and I communicated to each other through our eyes. Feeqa had become further disoriented when I saw him in the evening. I tried to calm him down, 'I haven't told anyone, and Mehr is not going to either. No one suspects you.'

The police carried out a cursory investigation. Blood was cheap in those days for murders had become an everyday affair. The knowledge of this secret made me feel like a big boy. 'Feeqa, I haven't even told mother.'

'Tell her if you want the entire neighborhood to

24

know,' Feeqa laughed.

Mehr had always been a man of few words. Swai Ram felt safer now, after Sheeda's death. Finally, Swai Ram was the sole casualty of our area in 1947. Dhurrey Shah had been breaking locks on the morning of 15th August . . . Among the Hindu shops, Swai Ram's was the only one open. He decided to lock it up. Dhurrey Shah was drunk. He came up and stabbed Swai Ram. This was the second murder I had seen within a week.

The whole world changed. I became a member of the National Volunteer Corps. Feeqa became loquacious. He would sing all night long. Walking around, he'd beat the rhythm on his water sack, *'akhiyan mila ke, jiya bharma ke, chale nahin jaana.'* Yet, he had changed somehow. Mehr told me six months later that he had taken to drinking rot gut. The affliction finished him off within a year. I moved from the city to Lahore and then I became a government officer. While on vacation I'd visit Mehr to buy fruit. His mention of Feeqa would bring tears to my eyes, 'Boss, a good man's life is tough.' Mehr was a good man too; he left the world quickly. Feeqa faded from my memory. Last night, he gave me the melon – an excuse to remember me and be remembered.

Translated by Moazzam Sheikh

Hero

I came to Lahore when I was appointed a Lecturer in 1953. The city had changed much since I had last visited. That had been before the tumult of the partition. Shahana, like me, was an outsider, but he was a true lover of the city. He would take me along as he indulged in various pleasures, stopping here for seekh kebabs and there for sweets. The city was taking on a new garb. Stylishly dressed men walked next to Lahori women with an air of intimacy. One spotted famous people too while ambling through the city.

I entered the old city via Mori Gate one day. People were busy with breakfast. It was still quite early in the morning. A sharply dressed man of around my age stood in a doorway, wearing neatly ironed pants and a dress shirt. I took him for a fellow lecturer or upscale clerk and greeted him with an air of familiarity. In reply, his salam was even warmer. "Come inside brother, enjoy some tea before heading out. I just brewed a pot. You will forget the foreign variety." I shook his hand, and he patted my shoulder and led me inside. "You must be heading to the office soon, please don't bother yourself on my account!" I said to him, "I don't go to any office. My wife and kids are still asleep. I'll have my tea and then wake them up," he replied.

Inside, a large room seemed to stretch before us like a street. He sensed my bewilderment and broke into a famous film song. *"This is god's abode, this is the temple of justice,"*[4] came the tuneful refrain from his lips. "This used to be a temple. In 1947, the more powerful took over houses left abandoned by those who fled. My father was a simple man. He came across this temple and found it empty. Just like you, he was amazed at how far the room stretched, as if there was no end to it. Later, we added some dividing walls ourselves, using bricks from the stairs we removed from outside."

"My name is Nadir Ali and I teach at Government College," I said, finally introducing myself.

"Sir, it is an honor to meet you. My name is Javed, but everyone calls me Jaida Hero because I am a film buff!"

"You do look like a hero. You have a hero's voice and personality." I didn't say this to flatter him. He really reminded me of one.

"Professor Sahab, they say a good customer at the very start of the day, and running into a good human being early in the morning, both bring good luck. Actually, I've been offered the chance to appear as a hero with Sabiha!"

"Javed Sahab, the good fortune is mine. I will be able to boast that I know the hero when the film comes out!"

"I am a kite-maker by profession. Let's see if my kite soars to new heights!" Javed added.

"Inshallah!" I replied.

I knocked on his door ten days later when I

---

[4] A song from *Amar*, a 1950's Hindi film

happened to be in the neighborhood. Hero emerged as if in a film reaching its conclusion. He had grown a stubble and his clothes were disheveled and dirty. "It seems like you were out late last night. How is the film going?" I asked.

"Professor Sahab, the film ended for me. My boss did not allow any pause in kite-making for four straight days as Basant[5] was upon us. The kite-flying festivities couldn't wait. I made it to the studios last Saturday only to hear the director say, 'I waited and waited for you Hero. Eventually, I cast someone who came via the producer.'"

"Oh no! What an unfortunate turn of events, Javed Sahab. God willing, you will get another chance."

"Professor Sahab, life is like the mail train hurtling forth. It skips the smaller stations." Hero was on the verge of tears. "A father who hauls a cart of stuff to sell at the market, a son who makes kites for a living, both are stuck in a quagmire. How impossible it is to break free!" "Don't lose heart Javed Sahab!" I said.

I made it a point to visit and check up on him every month or two. His speech and style were reminiscent of a hero and the well-ironed pants soon returned. He remained a fan of movies and his visits to film studios continued. I would bring up films in our conversations. "Your manner and appearance remind me of Dilip Kumar," I said one day. "That man really deserves to be worshiped, Professor! I am older than both you and Dilip Kumar. I have seen so many screen heroes. Chandar Mohan, Prithvi Raj,

---

[5] Traditional kite-flying festival at the beginning of Spring

Ashok Kumar, and plenty of others. But no one comes close to Dilip's stature in the whole world. You have seen English films too. Tell me, is there any other actor quite like him?"

"I too am a fan of Dilip Kumar and yours," I could not help saying in reply.

"You must be pulling my leg boss! *Cheh nisbat-e-khak ra ba asman-e-pak!*"[6]

"Have you studied Persian Javed Sahab?" I asked.

"I never went to school, but I mingle with the educated crowd. I memorize sayings and verses. I didn't even manage to send my kids to school. You could say one set of wheels on the car of my life was slow and I couldn't manage these things well. My eldest daughter is a grown woman now and the second one will be soon. Even my son is past the age for school. Some things are just fated to turn out this way."

Still, Hero was not one of those who gave up on life. I also kept up my visits. I attended his daughter's wedding too. It was a simple affair. Hardly four guests came from the groom's side and a similar number of Hero's friends showed up. Food was served and the bride was bidden goodbye. The mother and daughter hugged each other and cried. Hero stroked his daughter's head affectionately and said, "God be with you child. Don't cry, you are not

---

[6] The Farsi saying is "Cheh nisbat-e-khak ra ba aalam-e-pak" (How can the lowly earth relate to the holy world / realm?), but here the writer chose "Cheh nisbat-e-khak ra ba asman-e-pak" (How can the lowly earth relate to the holy sky) either knowingly or by mistake.

leaving town!" My association with him continued and he attended my wedding. Even among professors, officers and big landowners, the charismatic Hero stood out. No one dared to make him feel inferior just because he was from a different social class. If you ask me, all of life is simply the putting on of a performance. To be an officer or a powerful landowner simply means acting out that part.

Time passed and my black hair turned gray. With my somewhat comfortable lifestyle, I grew soft and flabby. But Hero didn't change. He still walked tall and erect like a soldier and spoke like an officer. I take that back, the comparison with officers is pointless. There was no one quite like Hero! Despite his age, his voice was loud and forceful.

His son managed to haul a cart of goods to sell each day and Hero's financial situation improved. But eventually, he suffered a blow as dramatic as the kite-flying festival. The government banned Basant!

"Professor, the raids on our business far outnumber any kites we make. We are making do with my son's earnings. You are well-versed in politics and follow news from around the world. Do you think Pakistan's film is about to end?" he asked one day.

"Films will continue, as long as we have our heroes," I quipped.

"The actors these days are pathetic, Professor. Now we have a television at home. Bhutto was our last great actor!"

At seventy plus years of age, Hero still manages to impress. We could be a proud nation if we elect him

President. His pants never lose their crease and none can match his dialogue delivery! Alas, we are not a discerning people!

Translated by Amna Ali

Nooran Niari

The old hag Nooran died at the age of ninety last Thursday. My elder brother announced we'd go to the funeral and our sister added, "How lucky of her to die on a blessed Thursday of the holy Ramadan."

"She died childless. How much longer did she plan on living? Once you cross eighty you might as well drop dead," I retorted.

"What's the matter with you, Noor? She was our mother's friend. You were even named after her," she admonished.

Come to think of it, what did I have against her? When I came of age, around the year 1946, my mother used to visit Nooran quite frequently. We were the goldsmiths, they the sand-sifters. My family had six shops in the Jeweler's Bazaar. My mother's folks were, on the other hand, ironsmiths from the city of Sialkot. The maternal side of my father's family insisted on the match because of her good looks. My father was a romantic at heart and in order to prove just that he fathered eleven children. But the paternal side of his family never ceased branding my mother an outsider. Only Nooran, the sand-sifter, acted like a relative to her. My mother would mention her in every other conversation.

"Oye you, Sialkot lass! Your parents must have thought: be Lahore-bound / then never be found!" The old hag's voice still rings in my ears. She was a storehouse of two-liners, proverbs and poetry, and the moment she spotted my mother, she'd holler, "Meher bibi, the goldsmiths don't count you as their own! Nizam Din and family can't know your worth! They don't even consider us humans. They are the goldsmiths, we the sand-sifters, lowest of the lowly. If you are the moon and the sun, then why call us the unique ones."

She had plain features and fair skin. And her eyes - big and wide, full of shine; half the time she'd let her eyes do the talking. She danced and laughed through her eyes. Newlywed, my mother was forced to listen to nonstop yarns about goldsmiths and ironsmiths. "C'mon, girl, don't waste your time listening to your golden in-laws. I have already wasted half my life listening to such nonsense at the Jewelers' Market."

Two days' absence was the limit, and Nooran, clad in her black burqa, would descend on our house; she'd never veil her face though and the moment she entered the portico she'd caste off the robe irrespective of the presence of men and women, since she considered everyone to be younger than her. Entering, she'd recite a couplet: "Bullah, let's go to the goldsmiths, where they craft a thousand ornaments / witness a thousand unique faces, yet behold the unique One."

As long as she stayed around, one felt caught in a tornado. The moment she left, there appeared sudden calm. "Oh god, when Nooran leaves, joy leaves with her," my mother would say wistfully.

I never liked her. Even when I was a baby, I'd wail

upon seeing her. Once I could speak, I took up the habit of calling her "Nooran the bear." My mother would try to humor me. Nooran too kept an orange or a candy with her for enticement. Yet, nothing worked. As I grew up, I added *dracula's heir* to *Nooran the bear*. It'd make mother cry.

I am forced to ponder now what lay at the root of it all that bothered me so deeply. I remember the day when my maternal grandfather died. He didn't enjoy much worth in my family's eyes. However, it is only normal for a family to weep together when someone passes away. Strange, everyone at my house remained a mute spectator. My mother cried her heart out. An aunt or two would comfort my mother occasionally. My father, similarly disinterested, was not much help either when he came home. "Let me go and get the tickets for the three o'clock train," and with those words he sneaked out.

Nooran clasped mother warmly when she arrived at the scene. She kissed her face. She took my mother inside the room. She even went to Sialkot with her. While my family returned right away, she stayed there for seven days. "She's Meher's own blood, don't we know that?!" my aunts would taunt.

What was my mother's relationship with her? Nothing except she loved looking after my mother. She could make Kashmiri tea in a flash and she could recite Bulleh Shah at will. Due to the tea and poetry combination, I made up the rhyme: "Bulleh Shah / Kashmiri cha."

Ah yes, it was in fact Abdul Sattar, the tailor's son, who'd planted the suspicion in my heart. "Oye Noor, have you noticed her husband? Cheema the sand-sifter looks her father's age. He is impotent. Something's fishy about Gulzar the wrestler. I think he's been sleeping around with her." "Gulzar, Nooran's yaar," I rhymed it up in my heart but could not share it with others. Finally, Sattar added a gem of a twist: "Nooran is a Mundaybaz." "What the hell is that?" I asked, bewildered. "Just as men do with men. Women carry on with women." He had more to say but I couldn't understand a whit. A kind of suspicion took root in me.

1947 had arrived. The city's name had become synonymous with murder and loot. Fear reigned as far as the eye could see. The Jewelers' Market closed down. Some Hindus sold whatever they could at whatever price possible and left. Those who were still around didn't open their shops. Gold was mostly sold at night. One day curfew was imposed on the city and people sneaked in and out within their own neighborhoods with discretion. That afternoon I realized mother was not home. When father asked about her, I said: "She must be at Nooran's. I'll hop over there via the rooftops."

I crossed four rooftops and finally entered the house from the stairs to encounter complete silence. I went towards the courtyard. "Who is it?" Nooran jumped, alarmed. Due to the heat, she'd covered herself with a sheet as mother lay next to her. Mother sat up – she was drenched in sweat, her face red.

"Your mother was scared. I said, Come lie down with me. It is I who should've been scared. Your uncle Cheema has gone to 'Karaanchi'. He must be

35

searching for gold in the ocean." Like a lying witness she continued talking and laughed. My mother remained tongue-tied.

"Nooran, mundaybaz!" I hollered as soon as I entered the living room of our house. My mother slapped me hard for the first time ever. I couldn't tell Sattar about the episode. He wasn't capable of keeping secrets.

Nothing had changed in Nooran. 1947 was the weirdest year. A knot had formed in my stomach. After Noor Jehan's superhit *Chanvay* was released, Nooran would sing *"Wey mundya Sialkotiya"* as soon as she spotted me. She'd pinch my cheek first and then my mother's. "Her heart is full of love," my mother would say.

It must be that. But I remained suspicious. In 1971 my mother died. Nooran cried an ocean, clasping me to her body. I felt relieved. Even at the age of ninety she had such a sparkle in her eyes. The old guard has by now pretty much died out. The rest migrated to upper middle class neighborhoods like Garden Town and Model Town, except for Nooran and Sattar. One day I saw the old man Sattar emerging from her house. "Oye, what took you to the house of the mundaybaz?" I asked, laughing. The old man replied, "No, Noor. The old bone is a good woman. She has helped me a lot all my life." May God keep her in peace. She was a kind soul.

Translated by Moazzam Sheikh

Saint of the Sparrows

Nurpur is now a city and no longer the small town that once hosted grand fairs. Shah Seyku's fair took place on the eastern edge of the town and Saint of the Sparrows' near the foothills. Shah Seyku's tomb now falls within the city limits and the fair has ceased. The heat of June's first Thursday feels intolerable and the village bigwigs have set up their mansions at the exact spot where the theater and circus once camped. A new police station has been erected where a book bazaar earlier made its home. No surprise when you realize that no one knows who Shah Seyku was. Village bumpkins like me would point out that in peak summer he indulged in soaking up the sun and lighting a fire; and if he took a fancy to throwing ash in your direction or cussing at you, your wishes came true. Come summer, the fair brimmed with people, smearing their sores with ash or taking it home to use all year long. The exact bustling point has given way to a health center. No drums were played nor did the fair take place last June. Sheikh Miraj Din, the historian of the city, tells us that Shah Sheikhu[7] in fact was buried here,

---

[7] The historian seems to think that the tomb was the burial place of Emperor Jehangir, also known as Shah Sheikhu and perhaps he counters the belief that there was someone else named Shah Seyku.

temporarily, while he was returning from Kashmir, before being shifted to Sheikhupura.

Our beloved Saint of the Sparrows died in 1925. The fair in his name still attracts quite a lot of energy on the third Sunday of the month of Sawan. From the southern end of the city, his *gharoli*[8] is carried out by his devotees, one of whom is currently an MPA and the Minister of Food. A large dancing crowd leads the procession. People make a ceremonial offering of fine cloth and distribute drinks sweetened with jaggery. There's a tiny jungle near the hillocks. The first rain of the month of Sawan is also counted among his miracles. The Saint himself is evergreen and he keeps Nurpur verdant too. There hangs his photo with sparrows at the shrine. He sits smoking a hookah in the photo, sparrows surrounding him and sitting on his shoulders. He used to feed them rice, millet, breadcrumbs. He lived on millet bread and drank goat milk most of his life; never ate meat. Cooked meat was not allowed at the fair either. Perhaps the town had a lot of Hindu residents. Meat seemed to be nonexistent in Nurpur. Even nowadays meat is not cooked in the houses of strict devotees.

The Saint of the Sparrows was one of a kind. The bread he ate was made from the flour of millet he grew in a little field. The milk he drank came from the goats he raised. Rain or shine, he wore the same loincloth, which he spun himself from the cotton he grew with his own hands.

---

[8] A decorated pitcher of water

People share a peculiar story about him. Supposedly he hailed from a large city, but barely uttered a word, except to little children and goats and sparrows. Among his devotees are the headmen of the area. Hindus, Muslims, and Sikhs visited him and continued to visit his shrine after he passed away. Womenfolk from lower castes and beyond would come by, though it was a rare sight to spot someone within close proximity of him. He would head towards the hills upon seeing people approach. Sitting, waiting, the supplicants would weep. Gradually a tradition evolved requiring people to sit far away, behind a cluster of berry trees later to be known as the Jungle of the Saint, the same spot where his shrine was built. There's a saying: *If the sparrow by flying away, makes the Saint downhearted, there will be no rain!* People sing it and dance the jhumar or drum on a small pitcher. Another saying carries the same ring: *The sparrow man laughed when the rains came, allowing Nurpur to breathe!* His symbols are soft and gentle.

The fair truly comes alive on the second day; no fights erupt throughout. A huge *kaudi* game takes place there and if it weren't for the blessings of the Saint of the Sparrows there would be bloodshed. His disciples, too, are blessed that way. Their family members also don't put on airs, even after becoming assembly members and ministers. When all is said and done, the inside story turns out to be quite different. During the fair at his shrine I heard the following from the twittering sparrows:

He was the king of beauty and the Alexander the

Great of conversation. He came from a poor household, but his temperament was that of a completely contented person. The headman of the city was much older than him, but he was the shining moon of his gatherings. He felt blessed and happy in many ways because of him, a natural settler of disputes, winning over both parties by telling right from wrong. Although the real power no doubt remained with the feudal lord Jalal Khan, the beauty and elegance of the Saint of the Sparrows held sway. In order to deflect the evil eye, his parents named him Rura. Instead of being a heap of rubbish, he turned out to be as dazzling as rubies. Intelligent and warm, his laughter and speech exuded beauty. Anyone who shook his hand would recover from a cold or fever.

Chance itself waited for the beautiful one! The lone daughter of Sardar Jalal fell in love with him, who was more like a family member to Sardar; but then he could enter any house as if he were family. Zeenat saw him drawing water from a well and seized the bucket from him. He drank from it, washing his face afterwards. Sardar witnessed the exchange from the upper window, which he faced, while Zeenat had her back to her father. His daughter seemed to be floating in a different world. She picked up the saint's slippers and brought them over and while he watched, she touched his feet. He was a mountain untroubled by wind or storm. He put on his slippers and on approaching Sardar he touched his feet and said, "Today I have come with a special plea. Accept me as your son!" No one knows who really witnessed this spectacle, but Sardar was nothing but a snake, his entire being becoming venom, erasing his sleep. Eyes red, inflamed, he kept the matter locked in his heart until he could strike at an opportune moment.

A gathering took place at the mansion. A few attendees broached the subject of Sardar's mood. Some enquired after his well-being, others indulged in flattery. The scene in the room foreshadowed a calamity. The Saint of the Sparrows stood up. "Sit down, Rura!" thundered Sardar. No one even remembered the name Rura. He used that name only when instructing others to let someone know that Rura had visited, but Sardar Jalal always addressed him as Lalu or Lal ji. People also chose to call him Lal saab or occasionally Lat saab out of love. "Oye, who picked you from the rubbish and turned you into Lat saab?" "God did make me Rura while the name Lat saab was chosen by you. I ask God's forgiveness because of that name," said the saint. Sardar leapt like an eagle and snatched the saint's dhoti, casting it away. "This too I gave you to wear and now I take it away!" God knows what else took place in that meeting, but not a bird chirped. The saint's forehead sweated and turned red as a beet. Sardar got scared when he saw him raise his hands as if about to strike him, but he grabbed his tunic and tore it before tossing it to the floor. He strode through the city naked. People couldn't muster the courage to look at him twice. The whole city grew obscured. He left, completely freed of clothes. People say it poured for three days and nights. The city sunk into waist-deep water, raising fears it would drown completely. The wall around the women's quarters of the mansion crumbled. As soon as the rain stopped, diseases spread everywhere. Sardar's daughter took off her clothes to jump into the well, the very spot where she had touched her spiritual husband's feet. Wails erupted throughout the mansion and rumors spread about Sardar's daughter having left to search for Lalu. The body didn't float up for several hours. Curtains were erected around the well. Carrying a sheet, Sardar himself climbed down the well with the help of a rope. Ten men pulled on the rope, but the wheel wouldn't turn. It took twenty men to do the job. The whole city cried up a storm when the funeral took place. She had shed all worldly attire before taking her life.

He was found asleep, unburdened by clothes, a hundred miles away in the servants' millet field; the servants informed the owners. People tried to speak with him. Some of them offered to lend him a sheet. He would not utter a single word. People tried every method to coax him out of his silence. He sat with his head between his knees. He lay down once the people left him alone.

Someone from the servants' home left bread and a pitcher of water near him. He chewed on plain bread. Drinking a handful of water, he proceeded to sleep in the corner. The servants left the pitcher there. Next day, the people found the pitcher smashed, and him gone. Yet the servants were fated to serve him. Searching, they went to the foothills and found him near the stream, asleep next to scattered jaman seeds. Jaman is found everywhere in the city and it grows wild in the jungle nearby. One of the servants fell in love with his face. When he returned the next day he fell at his feet, weeping with abandon. "The palanquin has left, never to return, despite your weeping," The servant Khadim Husain wrote that in a state of trance. Now the whole world knows of Khadim Husain's Punjabi poetry, but it was actually a gift from the saint. Khadim pleaded and kissed his feet, and that led to his eyes filling with tears. He patted his head gently and Khadim grew radiant. The saint asked feebly, "Do you need a naked servant?" "Look at the lucky Sohni who found a beautiful friend," are the words from Khadim Husain's kaafi created in such a mental state.

He made a cave by the ravine his abode. A throne of marble now sits there. The saint would till the land with a spade all night long. He grew millet and tobacco. He was self-sufficient in his needs, including his own hookah and fire. Yet he maintained his state and no word left his mouth. He plowed for four hours every night. Come day, he withdrew inside the cave to sleep. His hair and beard grew long. He became slim as a straw. "But how can you plead with someone who's never upset with anyone," asks Khadim Husain in another kaafi. At last, Khadim Husain begged him to put on clothes because women also came by to behold him while remaining obscured from his view; it's immodest. Only then the saint grew his own cotton to later pluck it and weave his own langoti, which appears in the photo.

Translated by Moazzam Sheikh

Bala Flatulent

One couldn't think of a single person throughout the Salt Range who might remotely resemble Raja. Six feet was a minimum recruitment condition by the Hong Kong police department. The old man was even taller by a handspan. Most of his life he avoided applying freshly squeezed oil to his head, yet when he returned home from Hong Kong after finally retiring, he brought six bottles of oil in his luggage. Folks of our background could've seen fragrant oil pressed in foreign lands only from a distance, but sometimes while oiling his skin, he'd offer, "Smell it and quickly close the lid." Then, as time passed, he would acquire a bottle of Amla Hair Oil every month or so, and regardless of a cheery occasion or otherwise, he always wore a spun silk tunic of the Two Horse brand, just as his head donned a turban of the same material on the occasion of eid or shab-e-barat. Prodigious Rajput mustaches reached his sideburns, not to mention a striking pair of shoes and a distinguished swagger stick in his grip, too, always.

People had no way of knowing the secret of him being a coward, a farter. Nor did he have any intention of letting others in on it. But then it so happened that on one occasion his elder sister pronounced him a farter and the word spread like fire. The village of Chupal Kalan seemed big only in comparison with other Chupal villages. In reality it was just a tiny dot where hunger performed bhangra dance wherever you looked despite so many of the men being army recruits. Hong Kong on the other hand paid handsomely of course, and yet there were times when the old man parted with money frugally although he always managed to dress and eat with style. Fragrance rose from his hair and aroma wafted from his kitchen when a whole chicken or a kilo of meat was prepared in honor of a visitor. It makes little difference to the starved if the masters are really farters. A few did taunt him as Bala Flatulent behind his back with little to no effect on the old man's sense of self-delusion.

One could count on one's fingers large sized horses found loafing around the Salt Range and once you reached the mountains for sure you rarely encountered one, sturdy or weak; that being the case, however, everyone longed to own a strong ox. As soon as the fair began, the oxen trade dominated the scene, although people would also bring along oxen and stud bulls past their prime. Stud bulls alone resembled the Rajas, all decked up with bells and trinkets while being escorted by men, front and back, the spectacle nothing short of beholding the arrival of a Raja's carriage.

Our Raja never went back to plowing his land, but he couldn't resist purchasing a stud much bigger in size, like him, than other farm animals. Raja stood apart from common people, and so did his animal, which could be picked out right away. I grew up watching the old man and the animal from afar.

Hard to tell if any of his sons or daughters resembled him, but his stud did bear an uncanny similarity to him. A lot of care and pampering was bestowed on the animal despite its infinite uselessness.

True, Raja saheb didn't give two hoots about tilling the land; interestingly the stud also turned out to be effete. Whenever from a neighboring village someone brought a cow, us boys would be holding our breath to catch the spectacle of fucking. We'd sit, our legs dangling from a wall or a parapet, even an upper verandah. The secret that Raja's animal too turned out to be just another flatulent revealed itself on a similar occasion. They had brought a cow from a neighboring village of Tarpal. The old man Raja tried to wiggle out saying his stud had just mounted a cow yesterday. I wasn't there on Monday, but I did witness the strange show with my own eyes on Tuesday. Raja's stud couldn't be coaxed into performing the act. They would take the animal for a quick walk and massage it too but it refused to mount. A handful of ill-nourished young male animals, unclaimed, always wandered in the open field. A young, malnourished bull suddenly came charging from a side of Heera Purni's house and mated with the cow. Raja once thought of hitting the intruder with his stick and the cow's owners also tried to push it off, but it all happened within a blink of an eye that the bugger covered the cow and was done gone. Covering should never take much time anyway. A laughter rippled through the boys. Raja steered his stud home as did the cow's owner to his animal. But people kept the story alive and, in fact, the story of Raja's remaining life became connected to that of his stud.

The stud bull might have been taken to the fair on the eid occasion a few times, but my recollection is vague. Eid holds meaning only for those who can afford clothes and have an animal to show off or enough money to cook a meal and invite others. The big man possessed all the eid paraphernalia such as clothes and turban; not to mention he made sure to have the stud fig up, too, for the rest of the eid day.

Morning, he'd send a lad to the village maulvi to inquire about the amount of *fitrana* he owed. Maulvi ji would figure out the amount of wheat and calculate the going rate and come midday, you could ask anyone either from Maulvi or Raja's family about the amount of *fitrana* coming from Raja's pocket. Raja ji would take his sweet time to reach the mosque while Maulvi kept sending the messenger with a word about worshippers awaiting him at the mosque. He'd dress up formally of course and the stud as well. He'd wear a turban and have the animal's horns oiled. At the mosque, Raja's dazzle would make the worshippers' attention shift from the qibla to the spun silk. Raja himself collected the money by walking through the lanes in the mosque veranda. Afterwards the people nearby would embrace Raja as people do on eid and sneakily glide a hand over the soft cloth. One must marvel at how God designed for so much toil in nature simply so we may experience softness.

It was probably the second or third eid when the stud grazed Raja. Four men had busied themselves with polishing its horns. Raja too stood at close range, leaning forward, witnessing the spectacle when one of the men screamed, "Watch out, Raja ji!" just as the blood spurted from his chin. What the hell, he did own at least half a dozen silk shirts while, alas, someone like me could not even procure one on the special occasion of eid. A man covered the wound with a burnt piece of cloth first, though later Raja brought out clean cotton. Eventually just a mark remained, but the wound did reveal the malady of diabetes Raja had kept secret. Despite the passing of many months, the wound on the chin would open up whenever he had his shave done. He would say, "*tazah khwahi dashtan een daagh hai thodi ra*," while cussing at the barber, "Motherfucker, can't you watch where your razor wanders to?' Finally, he took to doing his own shaves. Still the soap suds would turn red. One of the perceptive men suggested, "Raja ji, have your sugar checked." And sure enough that turned out to be the case. Why does this deadly malady snare our weak masters!? Everyone seems to catch this disease these days, blaming sugar intake, but back then sugar was not as readily available. Raja sahab would not even drink tea with brown sugar. But perhaps it was sugar after all, who can tell! Still it appears the stud finished him off, not the sugar. Akin to how people had no clue regarding his cowardice, one has to read that story between the lines too.

After bequeathing a gash the first time around to Raja's chin and because of its utter uselessness, people proposed, "Pass it on to one of the butchers."

In reality, Bala Flatulent too was only worthy of butchers' attention, yet being "Raja ji" imposed a facade. The stud bull was useless when copulation or plowing mattered. All it could show off was its height and size which could only benefit the butchers.

Both, in the end, met their destiny on the next eid when the animal exploded, and running wildly, ravaged the courtyard. Even though someone did manage to shut the door to the outside, the inside suffered a tremor. People used to say, "Silence veils an earthquake; animals shake and break." Raja didn't have the mettle to go near the animal. None might have witnessed him running for his life in the courtyard, but when the animal pinned him against the wall, all hell broke loose. The animal lifted him up on its horns before tossing him at the wall. Raja didn't die though it was a close shave. He didn't venture out to offer his eid prayers. Nor did he go to the fair. Half the village came to ask after his health instead. The animal was sold to the butchers the next day.

No one detected Raja's precise malady. A few days following eid, Raja began to amble about. People said, when he seemed under the weather, that there must be an internal injury, though he could not have survived four years if he did suffer one. Nor would he take to bed for four years simply as a result of an animal's attack. In fact, he died bit by bit just as prophet Jacob did, suffering from pangs of separation caused by his son Joseph's absence. Raja too fell when his animal did as it was nothing but a symbol of his conceit. His faith in himself crumbled once the stud was sold. Family members also got sick of his infirmity. In his last days, it depended on the person's mood or whim to offer him a spoon of water. They would bolt the door before leaving the house. Fatigue was etched all over his eyes. In the meantime, several eids came and went. Whether it is true or someone made it up but when Raja Bala passed away, someone heard him mumble, "Turn the bull away!" But all over the Chupal region everyone knew that Raja's life's last five years were synonymous with those of his stud. It was not the animal alone which killed him though. It was also the sorrow of the animal that finished him off.

Translated by Moazzam Sheikh

Balwant Kaur

From Bhatinda to Bombay, we made our home in many cities, during my father's tenure as a railway employee. Although I was born in Lahore, our family belonged to Sialkot district. My father, Lalit Kumar Gill, did not belong to any place as such, being Christian and a railway employee on top of that. He could be in Howrah at one time, Peshawar the next. Though familiar with every nook and cranny of the country, it was our move to Bombay that gave us our first jolt. It seemed like we had stepped into a foreign city. I completed my bachelors in 1946 from Bombay, a city that couldn't care less for religion. My father was offered a job at the McKinnon company and retired from the Railways. He even bought a house in Colaba and would say: 'If Lahore is a wonderful place in which to be born, Bombay is the perfect city to breathe one's last!' But consider my luck. All it took was two dances in the Gymkhana club with Khwaja Khizr Lahoriya and I found myself wedded to him. His family didn't manage to convert me to Islam, but from the time of my marriage, they always called me Nadira.

Balwant Kaur was a close friend and we mirrored each other in many ways. Her father, Kuldeep Singh Randhawa, arrived in Bombay for business. Like me, she was a woman of the Jat caste from Punjab. But a photograph of her seated on a horse appeared in a

Bombay newspaper, and the caption read: 'Is this young woman from Punjab or Paris?'

I joked with her. "Punjabi woman from the heartland, beware the perils of riding a horse. Some John Cawas[9] will carry you off with him, whip and all!" But no John Cawas was written in her stars. A Muslim fellow snared her too. Qooma the Kakezai from Kasur. He was well educated and even dabbled in English poetry. But just before their marriage, the mother of the groom-to-be voiced her reservations.

"Khwaja Khizar's nikah[10] to a Christian woman is acceptable. But your marriage with a Sikh woman is not allowed the same blessing!" Qooma made fun of Khwaja's ceremony instead. "Oh, the swamp wedding in which the witness was a toad!"

No nikah took place for him and Balwant. Truth was, Qooma's clan was scared of the Sikhs. Two of the bride's brothers were captains in the Indian army, both posted in Rangoon. A civil marriage eventually took place and Balwant Kaur became Bakhtawar Bibi. She even recited the kalima[11]. She appeared taller than Qooma the six footer when she wore heels that added to her already tall frame, and was a year or two older than him. She addressed most males, besides her husband, affectionately as "sonny". However, neither Qooma nor any other man in her life was worthy of her affection. And that is the story of Balwant Kaur's life.

---

[9] John Cawas was a stuntman and actor in Hindi movies.

[10] Muslim marriage ceremony

[11] A declaration of faith by a Muslim: "There is no God but God, and Mohammad is the messenger of God."

Kuldeep Singh's folks were not hot-headed like some Randhawas, ready to pounce without even an exchange of words. They were Bombayites, softened by their privileged lives. How much one suffers in life cannot be measured by the number of years one has lived. Carefree years pass by in a flash while sorrowful ones stretch out without an end. An entire lifetime seemed to pass between 1946, the year of my marriage and 1947, when we left for Lahore. Some good years followed. By the time my first son was born, Balwanti had already borne three children, two sons and a daughter.

Times were what they were, but we had managed to reach Lahore. My family did not come to Pakistan, however my in-laws treated me well. Balwant Kaur's story, though similar to mine, now took a different turn. Her in-laws were demanding from the start. We joked about it at first. The crow is so right about how the Kakezai folks can squeeze the life out of you[12], she would say. But her laughter quickly dissipated and she went from being Bakhtawar, the lucky one, to Wakhtawar, the one with endless worries. No one even remembered that she was once named Balwant Kaur. Her entire family lived in India. As for Qooma, the hunter, it never occurred to him that women were more than objects to use and possess. Balwant was simply a prized hunt in his eyes.

Qooma's true self remained hidden during the riots and upheaval of partition, while Balwant's good

---

[12] A disparaging saying about those of the Kakezai caste

nature initially charmed her in-laws. She did not shy away from responsibilities. Her heart had the strength of trees. She was happy around birds, trees and children. If she pined for her family, it must have been at some nocturnal hour, when she was all alone. She never let it on. Men were still addressed warmly by her, some as "son", others as "brother".

Little by little, times changed and so did Balwanti's world. Only during hard times can one differentiate between the good and bad. Qooma had expanded his leather business over the years but when he suffered a few losses, Balwanti was simply tossed to the wayside. Qooma struck up affairs with many women, even forcing himself upon the cleaning woman at the Miani Saheb graveyard next to their home. A vile male treats a female like his possession. He managed to win a prized Jati for himself when times were good. She herself was begging to be nailed. When love is absent everything turns to ashes. She found no true friend in a life burdened with responsibilities and children to raise. At home, all the women treated her like an outsider, calling her names behind her back.

In 1962, Qooma wrote to us, decrying the constant bickering at home. His business wasn't doing well. Khwaja and I tried to knock some sense into him, pointing to the harm that would come to his children if he left Balwanti. But we should have known better! The eldest son proclaimed: "Aunty, it would be best if mom left. There is no redeeming the situation now."

Qooma's sisters and sisters-in-law accused

Balwanti of having an affair with his seventy year old uncle. "I treat the entire family with respect. I would keep the old man company, but Nadira, you know how commonplace that is in our upbringing!" she said to me. Divorce followed nonetheless.

The impossible turns into possible. From being the darling of her parents and a beloved of Qooma for two years, now she belonged nowhere. Luckily, it helped that there were still those she had warmly adopted as "sons" and "brothers". Mahna of Model Town managed to shelter her for two years. In 1965, Qooma married for a second time and his motive for divorce became even clearer.

Khwaja and I often called on her. She didn't need any help. She had managed to save some money. She began teaching at a school in Model Town but could not handle the burden of loneliness. Her three sons and a daughter were like snakelings. Not once did they bother to check on her. Balwanti would often break down crying. She pined for her brothers and for Amritsar. The mail stopped coming after the 1965 war. She lost all contact. One cannot easily hop over the walls of time and separation. 'Who can reunite us with those who lost touch and those we lost to death', says Heer.[13] Once people lose touch, they might as well be dead for each other!

Qooma and Balwanti's daughter was to be wed in 1968. Though she was too young for marriage, Qooma wanted to rid himself of her burden. When

[13] Tragic heroine of Punjab's famous love story "Heer Ranjha", with the most well-known version being Waris Shah's *Heer*.

Balwanti heard the news, she rushed to my place in tears. She told me she had some jewelry she had kept especially for her daughter. She seemed hopeful that at least they would allow her to give it to her in person and bid her goodbye. Khwaja had remained friends with Qooma. I asked if I could take the bride-to-be for some shopping. I arranged for the girl to secretly meet her mother at my place. Upon meeting, both mother and daughter hugged and cried. Sometimes one cries from sorrow and sometimes to lament the beatings one has taken in life. She gave her daughter a generous amount of jewelry as a gift.

I went to Qooma's place to convince him that denying a mother the chance to attend her daughter's wedding would be a cruel thing to do.

Qooma replied, "Bakhtawar Bibi should do us a favor by staying away so as not to spoil our festivities. She didn't even spare the jewelry when she looted us and ran away!" I didn't know whether to laugh or cry, having witnessed the mother giving the jewelry to her daughter. The gold bangles given by Balwanti adorned her wrists even now, as she sat mutely by her father. Neither she, nor I could reveal that she had met her mother at my place. Balwanti's tears now flowed from an even deeper sorrow. It seemed as though she had given up. Her health deteriorated and her knees could no longer carry the weight of her tall, heavy body. I brought the ailing Balwanti to my place. We moved to Islamabad soon after and the move proved beneficial. Khwaja had two extra rooms added to our house just for Balwanti. She lived for thirty more years. Why does

God punish the sorrowful ones with long lives? She died in 1995. Before she passed away, I'd begun a daily routine of driving her to Shakkar Pariyan so she could enjoy the sight of flowers. She addressed the gardener as "my son." When I visited the place after her death, he asked, "How come the old lady is not here today?"

I began to cry. "She called you "son" and in the end, you were her only remaining relative. She had no one else!" How could he grasp the meaning? I myself could not make sense of it. In 1996, Balwant's son, who often missed her, perhaps due to being the youngest, visited the United States. From a contact in Amritsar, he managed to get the phone number for his mother's brother Amreek Singh Randhawa who had moved to California. When he called the number, Amreek Singh's sons spoke to him.

He told them, "I am Amreek Singh's nephew, Balwant Kaur's son."

"Father spent his whole life remembering his sister! He died last year. You should visit us in Los Angeles someday," one of the sons replied.

They sent him some gifts for their aunt. Balwanti's son never mentioned that she had passed away too. At least fifty years later, after death had snatched her from this world, she had finally found one of her own.

Translated by Amna Ali

The Newspaper

God only knows who spread the news inside the mental asylum that Nawaz Sharif[14] had reached Mecca Sharif. No one bothers to read the newspaper in the asylum, except for Ahma Briefcase Holder, named for incessantly clinging to his briefcase filled with papers he goes around collecting all day long. Sometimes the doctor allows him to read the newspaper. If Ahma finds a news item that he deems important, he clips it to store in his briefcase. The doctor ends up punishing his behavior by forbidding him from reading the paper for a few days. On those occasions, Ahma takes the clippings out of his briefcase and reads them aloud to fellow inmates in the evening, often leading to mayhem. The briefcase then ends up being confiscated by the warden. Ahma pleads with the doctor and usually succeeds in getting it back. If he fails, he makes a new one as a replacement.

How did Nawaz Sharif make it to Mecca Sharif from Attock? No one had the answer except, of course, Ahma. He was mister know-it-all! According to him, one underground tunnel went all the way to Delhi from Attock. Another tunnel connected Attock with Mecca. Nawaz Sharif escaped to Mecca with his entire family. The Saudi king showered him

---

[14] Former Prime Minister of Pakistan

with praise.

Alongside the good one, a very disturbing piece of news was also making the rounds, that Noor Jehan[15] had been killed and buried in Karachi. Ahma had not read the news item himself since his briefcase had been confiscated after the Nawaz Sharif episode. Sheeda Doctor lent serious consideration to that affair, solving the mystery finally with the help of lyrics from one of Noor Jehan's very famous songs - *"When he whispers my name softly, I die on the spot."* Indeed, she must have died because someone had uttered her name softly! Sheeda Doctor reached his conclusion based on a gut feeling.

When Ahma read the actual headline, he learnt that General Yahya Khan murdered Noor Jehan after inviting her to his house. Now Yahya Khan was going to be court-martialed, according to Basheera Soldier, also known as The Clue Finder, based on new information he succeeded in tracking down. The news regarding Noor Jehan touched a raw nerve. Many had lost their mind listening to Noor Jehan's songs. And a few secretly desired to marry her. Those newly admitted to the asylum were mostly fans of Madhuri Dixit and Aishwarya Rai, but now all the men were busy remembering Noor Jehan. Ahma carried in his briefcase some freshly-acquired colored photographs of hers.

Amidst the relentless barrage of news, Sheeda Doctor complained from his perch on a tree,

---

[15] Famous Pakistani singer

59

"Neither the news nor the bloody newspapers believe in taking a break!" Ahma issued a sullen rejoinder, "Who did you insult just now? Will your mother write the news if newspapers didn't exist?" "Yes, my mama will write for the BBC!" His Highness the Nawab of Bahawalpur clapped and crooned, "My Noor Jehan is gone, I am now forlorn! Nawab Sahab of Multan, Bahawalpur, Rahimyar Khan! You all share in my sorrow. To you I am deeply indebted. Now pray for the departed soul!" Nawab Sahab finished and raised his hands to offer a prayer.

The next headline Ahma shared was about the absence of wheat crop that year. "The Americans sent us seeds for barley instead of wheat this year. As you sow, so shall you reap!" The United States attacked Iraq that year. How prescient Ahma had been! When I visited the mental asylum, the entire city seemed to have been admitted there. "People have gone bonkers watching footage of the attacks on their televisions," the doctor there explained. Were people inside the asylum more insane than those outside? I could not tell anymore. Who is privy to top secrets - those inside or those outside, whose names we cannot name.

Translated by Amna Ali

Qissa of Shah Husain

*H*ow fitting to call the eleventh century an apocalyptic age, the rulers inept, the ruled starved. What can I really tell you about Lahore having visited it only once, my sixty years of life notwithstanding? Come to think of it, that hardly amounted to a visit. I reached Lahore after a journey of three days and nights. Night had already fallen when I arrived at Ram Nagar Ghat near Chandal Canal. Ram Nagar bustled with festivity day and night, yet Ravi Ghat was a picture of wretchedness. Ten thousand people toiled away on King Jahangir's tomb. Ravi Ghat was like a gate to Lahore, situated about two miles from it. Someone had aptly called it Shahdara, dar being door in Farsi.

As the saying goes, those from Jhang and Maghyana cannot comprehend Lahore, I too didn't see Lahore properly, so, son, how could I have met Shah Husain? They say seven hundred thousand folks make their bed in Lahore every night; a deluge of people moved to Lahore when famine struck. There are said to be temple kitchens, and some are attached to mosques, yet the largest of all is the royal kitchen, feeding one hundred thousand people. Two thousand royal ovens! Now, they also add that half the ration makes its way to the Subedar's house. These are all imperial preoccupations. People in Gujrat couldn't care less. I have also heard people say, Shahjahan's toadies flip lies into truth! Imperial falsehood! Seven hundred thousand in Lahore and the same number live in Shahjahanabad. As per the rumors, wheat is being sent off to Ghazni. No, my child, people here consume it. I have seen three ledgers myself. Ten years of famine and ten years of plenty. Now that's God's math. Both famine and abundance are from God, a trial imposed by Him.

It was from Maulvi Kalimullah that I heard the story about Shah Husain. From here to Lahore, one could not find a scholar like Maulvi Kalimullah. He'd always insist, if you want to see true Islam, Din Mohammad, then visit Lahore. Shahjahani door-mats are the same everywhere, Gujrat or Lahore. But those dervishes are a different breed. Maulvi would add, justice, knowledge, and kindness on God's floor; tyranny and sickness at an emperor's door! In God's house one is neither Hindu nor Muslim. All creation is equal and everyone is a human being.

Child, I witnessed King Akbar's reign with these very eyes. Although they say, Shahjahan is God's peace, that is not the truth. They used to say, there's no king like Akbar and no fornicator like Jahangir! That is just hogwash made up by people. Jahangir's known to have appeared for public viewing everyday, but who in reality has seen him? The eyes of common folk dare not settle upon kings. Every single day is the same, yet they are different each day. The poor wet their pants when the royal drum strikes. Monarchs inhabit a different world. Despite their claim to be from among us, they reside elsewhere. The saying goes, seven worlds and seven skies are ruled by Shahjahan. The famine lasted ten years. Shahjahan spent his nights sleepless for those ten years, the king's puppets insist.

Maulvi ji used to point out that it was all pointless chatter. He'd add, a king doesn't go hungry, but he indeed dies unfulfilled. And silly tongues might also pronounce that even people don't die of hunger. The famine hovered for ten years. He'd ask rhetorically, where would the grain disappear to? The proverb goes: thieves roam in the marshes while food is found in Lahore!

The real story of Lahore, however, remains synonymous with Shah Husain and Shah Husain's story is all about the famine. To sing Shah Husain is to experience rain. Be it famine or a time of plenty, he who listens to him turns joyous. Shah Husain's songs made people buoyant simply because he suffered along with them.

He didn't have a line of descent from the Prophet. He was the king of people's hearts. Seven hundred thousand mourners attended his funeral. They say it rained for three days and nights. The river Ravi lashed out at Lahore. Rumor has it that the princesses wept by the river's edge and begged O Allah, spare Lahore from drowning.

Today Shah Husain rests in the East and Data Ganj Baksh the West, however, back on that day it was recorded in the royal annals of Akbar's reign: He was intoxicated, and convulsing, he died at a prostitute's place. The people knew it unfolded at the old police station. The king's men grabbed hold of his feet and pushed him off the fort's wall. An earthquake shook the earth. All of Lahore rushed out of their homes. Someone wailed, Shah Husain has passed away! They couldn't have seen such a quake before. Forts shook, royal turrets fell, in Delhi the throne shuddered. As the saying went, o simpleton, no one can suppress me today! akin to what Shah Husain himself used to sing.

These days the inhabitants of Lahore and Kasur - two imperial outposts by the banks of Ravi and Sutlej respectively - sing the verses of Shah Husain. Hundreds of millions of people love him and find peace by invoking his noble name.

Being the only son, his parents had named him Husain with tenderness. He chose the name Madho when people taunted him for his friendship with a Hindu, Bhag Shah, whose son Madho became Shah Husain's spiritual second-in-command. Bhag Shah and Madho were his followers. Both father and son belonged to a merchant caste. Bhag Shah became the most prominent sweetmeat merchant of Lahore, setting up eye-popping shops with lavish displays of maida, misri, makhana, maakhiya. As the song goes, one added poison to sweets and the other turned poison into sweets. I can't comprehend, I just can't comprehend. People said they detected an allusion in it: to the one who hailed from Ajodhan, Baba Farid Ganj Shakkar, the protector of Pak Pattan, known as Shah Husain's spiritual master.

Very few are able to decipher the essence of a word. Swai Shah is credited with converting people in Kalukyan to Islam. He's the patron saint of our village. Today there are about a hundred and fifty households and two mosques both due to Maulvi Kalimullah. He guided and educated people. Swai Shah, on the other hand, barged in here in all likelihood with the Pathans. Not sure of his real name either. That part about being a descendent of the Prophet might also be unreliable.

Shah Husain, contrarily, rules the five rivers, with people singing his verses from Beas river to Sindh river as they discover God's path. Nowadays out of a hundred and fifty households, forty belong to the Hindus and four to Balnathiyas, who are neither Hindu, nor Muslim, and Lahore as well has Balnathiyas by the thousands. Bhag Shah, too, was an adherent of Balnath, I hear. People accused Shah Husain of being a Muslim by day and a Balnathiya by night.

He was a handsome prince hailing from a leading Rajput clan, and a hafiz-e-Quran above all. But his forever happy heart despaired when famine struck. In Lahore nothing but fights, politics, a kingdom splintered into a hundred! as the chatter goes. A dark night of famine stretched from Sindh to Ravi. The famine appeared differently in the villages and differently once you touched the alluring Chenab river. A different world existed after crossing the river. A journey of about three hours and you would find yourself in the land under the sway of the Chattha clan. A different world breathed under the Gondals and a different world under the Chatthas and Virks. The hanging of Dullah Bhatti of Pindi Bhattian took place during Shah Husain's lifetime. The politics of Lahore as a seat of power underwent

65

a metamorphosis. Delhi clasped Lahore, the wise ones noted. People said the beggars would give the benediction, I beseech God, may your nose ring and bangles never be removed! That was neither Lahore's vernacular, nor custom. That manner of speech and the saying belong to the bandits of Delhi.

Lahore was a bustling city before the famine. No division between Hindu merchants and Muslim rulers. All were God's creatures in his view. But to rule is to rive as the saying goes. When he was accused of apostasy, he shaved off his beard and mustache in the custom of the Balnathiyas. The entire country sang his lyrics. He would wear ankle bells and dance near the Red Well. Boys and girls from all over the city played under the banyan tree nearby. He would sing to the children and bring them sweetmeats from Bhag Shah's shops. He spoke softly and sang mellifluously as per Lahore's tradition.

He was finally arrested. The police chief had been his class-fellow and the judge his teacher. The royal verdict stated: Hang him for he indulges in politics! He incites the newly arrived from the villages. The judge disagreed and wanted witnesses to weigh in. The royal spies couldn't think of anything better than additionally accusing him of having an illicit relationship with Madho. *Astaghfirullah*, we seek your forgiveness, Allah! His followers would take out processions zigzagging through the city all the way to the court. Nervousness spread. The judge asked, Tell me, Husain, why do they call you Madho Husain? Why add the name Madho? The judge wanted to know why he sang *Inside and outside Lal reigns supreme.*

Laughing, he replied, I subdued the rulers, the Bhags and the Lals subdued me.

The judge asked, What's your religion?

Pat came his reply, The color of cotton is the same everywhere; I seek the God who belongs to the people.

God have mercy! the judge exclaimed.

He said, The god of kings is different. The Judge sings the praises of kings.

During cross examination witnesses were brought forth to make a case against him for indulging in homosexual behavior. That night passed quiet as death, a premonition of something about to befall. Hundreds of groups congregated in Lahore and Kasur. The largest was that of Shah's malang followers which took place near the village of Ichra. In village of Theh, his special disciple Alliya, who became a singer despite his Sayyad background, suggested murdering Madho.

Madho himself would have given his life for Husain happily, but that was against Husain's philosophy since he never killed even a fly, or spoke impudently with anyone. Our sangat commit a murder? Have we become like the servants of the kings, O heartless souls? His guru thundered, Some-one should go ahead and kill me to wash away the stain of accusation against Shah Husain saheb.

Alliya spoke again, Let's ask Shah Husain then. But who'd dare ask him, who could risk being called a traitor? Alliya said, I'll announce to him in the court that I have killed Madho. Let's see what the Teacher says.

Next day he whispered into Shah Husain's ear, I've killed Madho. Shah Husain's hands were cuffed and feet chained. He was the kind who had never spoken loudly, never hit anyone, now smacked Alliya's face with both his hands. Aliya crashed facedown, blood oozing from his mouth and nose. The entire court fell silent. Then the crowd chanted Allah-u-akbar! and Ram nam sat hai!. Dumbstruck, the judge shivered, unable to handle the fury. Muslims and Hindus began singing separately:

Let us speak of union, come let's go to the fair
Ram's name in the heart, come let's go to the fair

Everyone then sang as one voice just as the city of Lahore had always done. In the end, we all die, come let's go to the fair. The judge and the chief of police lost control of the court; the rulers felt the empire slipping. The judge rushed home. The city sang all night long:

Let's visit the Kheres' village, seeking union
with the beloved
Enter the fort by smashing its walls, craving
union with the beloved

And countless other songs rose as if Shah Husain was getting married. Horse riders galloped to Delhi fearing a rebellion in Lahore. The king said, Let him go! The queen overheard and asked, Tell

68

me whether he's a man of miracles? Is he good looking? The messengers were disciples too. One of them said, Lady Queen, the eye cannot linger long on his personage. The one he holds in his gaze becomes beautiful. Everyone chimed in.

Shah left the Red Well and made his abode in the Shahi Mohalla among prostitutes, who sang his verses. Drunkards and clients would return home repenting and singing his songs. Paying a visit to the Diamond Market is nothing short of a pilgrimage, someone sang, the Shahs know the secret to washing away sins.

In the darbar of Shah Husain there was already no Hindu, no Muslim. Now the distinction between the sinner and the virtuous vanished too. People said, When humans connect, monarchies crumble. The king ordered the secret police to have him killed. They arrested him, again, at night and tied his hands behind his back before tossing him off the fort's wall. The three soldiers went blind and jumped after him.

When seven hundred thousand people came for the funeral, Bhag Shah had already been dead ten days. Madho led Shah's funeral. Tears fell ceaselessly from his eyes. Everybody sang:

Return, my love, come back today
My love, don't you forget us

Whosoever beheld Madho that day fell in love with him. Many stories were spun hereafter. One he was remarkably beautiful, two a reflection of another beautiful one. People saw Shah Husain's face in his. The royal puppets, Shah Jahan's boot lickers, spread the rumor that he was Shah Husain's lover. But neither in Lahore, nor in Kasur, did anyone pay any heed. They continued to sing his songs. Ten years of plenty followed. Shah Husain did not return. Come, people, pray there isn't another Shah Husain.

Translated by Moazzam Sheikh

Mangta the Sarangi Player

This story appears to be more about Nawab Colonel Yaar Mohammad Khan than Ustad Mangta Khan the sarangi player. The only thing worth mentioning about Ustad Mangta's life is that he was the last sarangi player of Pakistan. No one makes or plays sarangis anymore.

Ustad Mangta was nearly my age. When we were children, Ustad Mangta's father, Ustad Allah Nawaz Khan had been reduced to begging. He was almost blind. Donning a big turban, he would come to our alley to occupy the steps of Bhagmal's mansion, which came to be known as Colonel Saheb Mansion, and play his sarangi, *"There's no peace or calm for me in this world."* Each of us would drop a coin into the sarangi. Even back then no one respected art in Kasur. Noor Jehan[16] had moved to Bombay. Allah Nawaz would brag, "She used to be my student as a child." But, then, every musician in Kasur claimed to be Noor Jehan's ustad. Mangta would have remained a beggar had his father not saved him by packing him off to Lahore.

This story is about the time when Mangta was still in Kasur, visiting and playing music at the so-called Colonel Saheb Mansion. Colonel Saheb took on the pretense of a nawab after arriving in Kasur, but he

---

[16] Leading playback singer before and after partition.

71

turned into a real nawab only after he became a member in Ayub Khan's election and later the Health Minister of West Pakistan on Ayub Khan's recommendation. It was rumored that he had indulged General Ayub Khan in 1947.

Colonel Saheb's story was not unique in itself and Mangta knew a lot more about it than other people. Colonel Saheb was in fact a non-political person and he could not have won even the union council election if it were up to him. Colonel! Yaar! Mohammad! He was neither a politician nor a nawab, neither a colonel nor a Khan. He belonged to a Sheikh caste and worked as a timber contractor in a state near Kangra. The Raja of that area appointed him as an honorary Captain of the state's army when the war started. He elevated himself to a major when he arrived in Hoshiarpur and then Nawab Colonel Mohammad Yaar Khan by the time he reached Kasur. He got himself allotted the Bhagmal Mansion, which was the largest in Kasur. He didn't have a penny to his name and was often seen reading a newspaper at Asghar's general store. Asghar was his only friend and it was due to the credit he extended that the household was able to squeak by. Asghar would read the paper regularly. The other day, Colonel Saheb was heard saying, "Asghar is my mentor in politics." Mangta retorted, "It's like how my father brags about being Noor Jehan's teacher." So I asked . . . and only then Mangta narrated the story of the Colonel Saheb Mansion's bleak days.

"There would be nothing in the house to eat, but

we two mirasis[17] could be found in his bedroom every night playing music to lull him to sleep. Nawab Saheb knew not a thing about music, yet since he had arrived in Kasur a mirasi or two would be in the bedroom playing music. He used to say that music was his soul's food. We would ask, 'Your Honor, what should we do about the other kind of food?' Nawab Saheb would say, 'Talk to Madam in the morning,' before conking out.

Begum Nawab Yaar Mohammad Khan, may God bless her soul, managed everything from household expenses to mowing of grass to cordial relationships with neighbors and friends. I went and told her that Nawab Saheb had sent me to ask for our wages. Begum Saheb in turn sent me off with a note to Asghar's shop. Asghar Saheb prepared two bags of various items. He asked me to take one for Begum Saheb and keep the other one. The bag contained garam masala, tea leaves and two seers of sugar. My mother was thankful for getting at least something."

"Fortune smiled on you," I laughed.

"Sir, there is only one problem with credit. No one extends it," Mangta drifted into a lesson on economics.

"So Asghar the shopkeeper was Saheb's friend and his generosity knew no end?" I asked. "No, Sir, the credit was renewed again only after he became a member and then a minister. In fact, it was Asghar who suggested, and paid the fare, so he could visit General Ayub in Karachi when Nawab Saheb was

---

[17] In India and Pakistan, mirasis are the genealogists, singers and dancers of various communities

penniless and used to read the paper at Asghar's shop."

"Then Asghar was indeed Nawab Saheb's teacher in politics!" I said laughing. "Not at all, Sir. The real teacher was the saintly Begum Saheb!"

"How so?" I inquired.

"Nawab Saheb would have sold the mansion, Sir. It was 6 acres of urban land and since the creation of Pakistan, the price of one marla had climbed to one thousand rupees. But it was allotted land and could not be sold . . . Later he somehow managed to sell the same land for 6 million rupees when he moved to Lahore."

"So he became a real Nawab thanks to the land!" I got myself entangled in economics again. "No, Chaudhery Saheb, a human being is the real wonder created by God." Mangta now turned into Plato.

"If Begum Saheb was not there, nothing would have been possible. Chaudhery Saheb, a woman who can make a mirasi mow the grass, she is capable of anything."

"Cows do need grass after all, Mangta," I said.

"No, Chaudhery Saheb, satisfied with the previous month's experience, I went to Begum Saheb again for my wages. She handed me a sickle and asked me to mow enough grass to fill three or four sacks. I said, Madam, a sword doesn't look good in the hands of a mirasi. But Begum Saheb showed me with her own hand how to pull the grass. Embarrassed, I mowed several mounds of grass till evening. She brought out a big sheet and asked me to take the whole thing to the bazaar to sell. It was worth four rupees. She kept two for herself and the other two she gave to me.

"Sir, I am Mangta but I have never begged for food. I have always worked for it. My teacher, doubtlessly, was Begum Saheb. If one could maintain a facade of being a Nawab by selling grass, one can achieve anything with some effort. Moreover, oh God, so generous! She split the money evenly. And, sir, when a person eats half of a roti and gives the other half to her servant, then the servant would not even think twice before sacrificing his own life for her."

Ustad Mangta was truly a teacher. He knew the art of speaking as well as the art of music. That is how he narrated the entire story of Colonel Saheb in bits and pieces and signals and signs.

Today Pakistan's last sarangi player Mangta Khan has died. Noor Jehan, the truly supreme singer, has passed away too. Most artists have vanished, but colonels and nawabs and ministers are still a dime a dozen. Finally, the story comes to an end without the artists. People do not understand that if Mangta had not been my friend, I too would not have been a writer.

Translated by Amna Ali and Moazzam Sheikh

Hussaina Qaachu

*H*umans will go on weaving endless stories, provided there are willing listeners who have the luxury of time. There may not be much to praise in a jail, but one can bet on hearing truly colorful stories. The people themselves are a colorful crew of thieves and murderers, villains and victims. Some are epitomes of misery and others surprisingly carefree!

At his own job, Baba Khazanchi[18] managed to rob the government of 20 lakh rupees ten years ago. He was sentenced to prison, but the money was never recovered. He made sure it never would be.

He would say, "I prefer prison to a life of tribulations! My family is better off this way." His close friend evaded authorities and managed to send money to his family every month. "That is all I am capable of, Malik Sahab," he would say. He adopted the habit of performing the ritual prayers five times a day and lorded over the prison as if he was the police officer. The other cheerful prisoner, Hussaina Qaachu, I was already familiar with from before his prison days. People had nicknames for all the hoodlums in town such as Jumma Bastard, Kaido Lame, Sujana Deformed, Phajja Stag! Hussaina Qaachu,

---

[18] A nickname, hoarder of treasure, given in jail because of his crime of robbing.

however, really was an expert chaaqu[19] wielder.

He was fearless, spirited, quick. All politicians needed a henchman like him. I would run into him often when he joined my circle of Cheemas. When I was appointed to the prison, Baba Khazanchi mentioned that one Hussaina from Nurpur, sentenced to hard labor, would make a good assistant for me. I realized he was the Hussaina I already knew, though changed into a more benign version of himself and no longer the tough guy the whole town knew and feared. Perhaps his slim build was the only hold-over from the old days.

I mingled with politicians now and then, and their henchmen always seemed to be lean machines, just like Hussaina. A heavy build is only good for lifting heavy weights. What we really need is a partnership of the mind and the heart. Even the heart needs a quick-thinking mind so one strikes at the most opportune moment. A slender, quick thinking fellow avoids getting pummeled. Even when it comes to being an adept horse rider, the slim one has an edge. A big mouth and big build are just bluster, nothing more. Most political leaders can intimidate with their heavy builds, mimicking jail wardens. But the real work is accomplished by those of Hussaina's ilk.

"Sir, you are perfectly built for our line of work!" Hussaina proclaimed, since I too am on the slim side.

"What job are you considering me for?" I asked.

"I am the one you need to call on. Consider me at

---

[19] Translator decided to keep the Punjabi word chaaqu for knife because of the wordplay with the name Qaachu.

your service for anything you need done!"

"How about going into politics?" I continued with my teasing.

"By the grace of God, I have helped many others become politicians in Nurpur!" he shared.

"How did you end up in this place? You've been handed a five-year sentence I hear."

"I would have come here much earlier had I known, sir. I am at peace here. I don't have the desire for any more encounters with the police! The Chaudhrys were ready to have me killed. I am much better off as a guest of the authorities!"

"How could the Chaudhrys think of having you killed after all you did for them?"

"It is how their kind operates, sir. They would get their own fathers killed if there was anything to be gained. Pardon my vulgar language, but they wouldn't think twice about selling their own mothers!"

"Hussaina, you are proving to be a wise chap!" I chuckled.

"I was a good student once upon a time, Malik Sahab, though my own folks were uneducated. I have no regrets about never finishing school. What good would it do anyway? At best, I would be a clerk at the District Commissioner's office. As it turns out, the District Commissioner is the one doing my bidding!"

"How did you manage to charm the District Commissioner?" I asked.

"With the help of the choicest mangoes, sir! It is a mistake to assume the rich have no desire for the small, seemingly ordinary gifts of life. You see, the price of mangoes happens to be quite high these days. I presented as a gift to the DC six baskets of mangoes I had picked with my own hands, the likes of which he had never seen before. He sent for me just to say that my mangoes passed his test. It took just one meeting with him and his wife and I became a household name.

"I would deliver mangoes and meats and vegetables of the highest quality to their home. I even made my way to the wife's family in Lahore. They are good people and treat me like their son. I made sure the deliveries to Lahore were timely and of the highest quality. Soon, everyone in the DC office greeted me warmly. DC Sahab visited the Secretariat recently and put in a word for me to the head jailer. It took one phone call from him and I became a free man within these confines. This prison too operates like a big business. I could make millions if I was a drug dealer! But even those who peddle drugs are scared of me. I am not the greedy kind." Hussaina revealed a new version of himself to me.

"What other talents do you possess, Mr. Political Genius?" I asked

"I am an excellent cook, sahab. I asked them to deliver some bittermelons today, just so I could prepare them for you."

I was taken aback at the sudden focus on me. "But my food comes from home every single day, Hussaina."

"My dish will be nothing like that food! I see you

sitting and reading all day long. Indulge in some food and drink for a change. I know you enjoy whiskey. Just say the word and I can order a foreign label. I still hold some sway in this city!"

"Good thing I have a few days off from work," I said, enticed suddenly by the thirst within me.

"Don't give up drinking just because of the obstacles! I imbibed much of the English variety. DC Sahab convinced me to quit because I got drunk and crossed a line once. I apologized, but he was adamant."

"DC Sahab himself is quite the drinker!" I commented casually."

Being childless is not easy on him. His wife is a wonderful person, but I think he has lost his heart somewhere else!"

"Who told you?"

"I am a very good reader of people, sir ji!"

"Have you ever lost your heart?"

"I did get married once, with Cheema Sahab's help." For the first time I noted a hint of sadness on Hussaina's face.

"What happened then?"

"I came face to face with the most beautiful human being I had ever seen. I fell in love with my own wife. But soon the hammer came down. How could I have known the Chaudhrys were merely using me? My wife also considered me beneath her. My heart broke. I should never have married. I never wanted a family anyways. Now only the pain lingers!"

"Why did the Chaudhrys want you married, Hussaina?" I got further entangled in the story.

"They were assuring my loyalty to their clan. My wife had other plans. She embroiled herself in intrigues. I tried to reason with her. But she played politics like a pro and greed deluded her. She would not rest till I handed over each day's earnings!"

"She probably wanted to see you rise in stature. Isn't that desire alive in every wife's heart?" I asked just to cheer him up a bit.

"Sir, as for a heart, she had none. She belonged to a caste of witches!" He became visibly more upset.

"Well, the Chaudhrys themselves are no angels, Hussaina!"

"Malik Sahab, you hit the nail on the head. I was a rookie and didn't understand. Perhaps being educated would have helped! I realize my mistake now. I have made peace even with this prison. People swindled me several times, but I am not a complete idiot. My happiness lay in serving my parents and friends. I am a happy man, thanks to your blessing."

"The world that awaits you outside is the same old minefield," I replied with genuine sadness.

"Sir, I plan to fake insanity. I have it all planned out. I have the blessings of the Almighty. Taste the bittermelon dish I cooked for you today! I have ordered mangoes too. They'll arrive tomorrow. You must have some."

Surely this Hussaina Qaachu could slay one even without a chaaqu!

Translated by Amna Ali

Bundu, Consoler of the Rich

I had a peculiar dream last night. I am the kind of man who always thinks deeply about dreams. When I lost and then initiated the arduous task of recovering my memory, I went in search of all those times I could not account for by raking through my dreams. We rarely make sense of the surreal glue that holds dreams together, reconstructing them as if they are stories. Indeed, sometimes they chronicle our longings, other times they unfold our ardent desires reaching fulfillment, as in the union of a man and a woman! In essence, words lay the foundation, not only of the inner world, but also of our dreams. Words illuminate this journey we undertake in the pitch dark. They help us penetrate the maelstrom of existence!

This is how the dream began. I address a seated man, apparently a doctor, as Shahabuddin. He transmutes into a woman when I sit down across from him. She has the most beautiful eyes. Dark-complexioned, she appears to be Bengali. I find her very attractive. We take a stroll to the front of the Zamindara College in Gujrat. I point out Nawab Sahab's grave to her. She moves closer to me as we approach the college hall. We continue on to the back of the college. My heart turns tranquil as the dream fades.

I did not have to venture far to find the rungs that

would help me comprehend my dream. Ah, I had recently read the translation of the Musaddas by Sir Shahabuddin. Since Shahabuddin had dark skin, he visited my dream as a woman with dark complexion. Again, it was he who dissolved into Balo Jati in my dream because he belonged to the Jat caste. I rushed to Balo and narrated the night's dream.

"Lady, I have to remove curtain upon curtain to find you, even in my dreams!"

She laughed and explained, "Such a distance lies between an old man and his youth!" I persisted with my interpretation of the dream. "I showed you Nawab Sahab's grave to indicate that I am old and decrepit, yet I live on, like Nawab Sahab's name lives on. We went to the back of the college to excavate my youthful days."

"Lahore, Chaudhry Sahab, is overflowing with young lovers. My most prized beloved, though, remains this old man. He is a parent and lover rolled into one. People need conversations to share our joys and sorrows, no? Who would I converse with if I don't see you Chaudhry Sahab?" Balo's words lifted my spirits. My dream bestowed its blessings and then was forgotten. Two months passed.

Yesterday, as I sat reading the biography of Khwaja Muinuddin Chishti - the Consoler of the Poor[20], Bundu Dhobi[21]appeared in my thoughts out of the blue. Consider that one of Khwaja Sahab's miracles

---

[20] Also known as Khwaja Ghareeb Nawaz (Consoler of the Poor), he was a sufi saint and founder of the Chistiya Sufi order in the early 13th century

[21] A *dhobi* is a washerman

or the secret of caring for the crushed! My mind recalled the two month old dream. I pictured the dark-skinned woman's eyes. Ah, exactly like Bundu's! So the woman was in fact Bundu the washerman!

Bundu is the only person I remember fondly from my two-year stint as a professor at Gujrat's Zamindara College. He transformed me into a Sahab during those youthful days of surviving on the pittance I was paid as a novice professor. I wore the best starched and brightest white shalwar kameez in the entire college.

I also happened to be the college hostel warden. One day, Bundu appeared with a plea. "Sahab, it is impossible to find accommodation in the homes seized after the exodus of the Hindus from the city. The Neighborhood of the Untouchables too is under police control. They have escorted so many women there, turning it into their own personal cantonment. It is indeed not befitting for real men to spend nights at the police-station! Please get me a place at the hostel, I will manage."

I arranged. lodging for him at the hostel. Meanwhile, I found it hard to manage my expenses after sending two hundred and fifty rupees home each month. I had rashly jumped on the marriage bandwagon too. I ended up renting a house in Madina village situated on the outskirts of the town. Bundu would walk the two miles to my place. I had a bicycle at least. Bundu never learnt to ride. "It has a mind of its own! What if the damn machine decides to carry me to Momdipur from Madina village?"

Bundu would tease.

The marriage ceremony and other expenses drained us of all our money within a month of marital bliss. One day, my wife announced, "Someone named Bundu Dhobi is asking for you." I stepped outside to meet him. "Sorry Bundu, I am penniless this month. I won't be able to pay you," I told him. "Sahab, I am not here to receive my payment. I am here to pick up the dirty laundry. Moreover, I haven't even congratulated you on your marriage. Your wife is one lucky woman. A good man usually finds a good match."

Little by little, Bundu developed the routine of picking up our laundry from my wife multiple times a week, instead of once a week. Thanks to the care he showered upon our clothes, my wife and I climbed up the social ladder. When the college let him go, he managed to rent a small place that used to belong to Hindus in Muhammadi village. We remained broke.

One day, my wife took out some old bills. "Bundu heard us fighting about the expenses. He left thirty rupees with me." I expressed my anger. We didn't have a penny. How were we going to repay him given how impossible it was to borrow from anyone in our village?

"He said we could repay him after one month. He placed the money in my hand." My wife tried to allay my worries.

Bundu played an important role in my transfer to Lahore when our principal accepted a position at the university and took me along. "You are the best-dressed man in all of Gujrat!", the principal had said.

From Lahore, I went on to Dhaka University in 1965. My children and I took to Dhaka, but luck was not on our side. We were spared the perils of detention in 1971 as we were able to come to West Pakistan for the summer holidays. But I remained affected by 1971. I became very ill. I lost my memory during treatment. Once recovered, I made a trip to Gujrat after a gap of twenty-five years. Bundu had passed away by then.

Today, Khwaja Muinuddin, the Consoler of the Poor, reminded me of my Consoler of the Rich, a most loving and kind-hearted man. Perhaps even Khwaja Sahab had been softened by such love from people. After all, a poor person can also be a benefactor of the rich! Such are the links of love. The foundational bond, too. As in the love between a man and a woman! In my dream, he appeared as a beautiful, dark woman. He was a very handsome man. How can I ever forget his deeply telling eyes?

Translated by Amna Ali

Biographical Note

Nadir Ali was born in Kohat on April 26, 1936. He received his early education at Normal School, Gujrat and then attended Cadet College Hasan Abdal before joining the army in 1958. He served three tours with the Special Service Group and was also an instructor in the Pakistan Military Academy. In 1971, he deployed to then East Pakistan and served with 3 Commando Battalion before returning to West Pakistan and retiring soon afterwards on medical grounds. He began to write in Punjabi in the 1980s. For a few years he migrated to the US with his family, but for the last twenty-five years of his life, he lived and wrote in Lahore, Pakistan. He died on December 26, 2020 and was buried in Machiyana, his ancestral village near Gujrat.